HOLT CLARKE

SWITCHING MAMA'S ASHES

Cover Art Illustrated by APRILILY

Imagination 2 Creation Publishing

Charleston, SC

Books by Imagination 2 Creation Publishing may be ordered through booksellers or by contacting:

Imagination 2 Creation Publishing
www.HoltClarke.com

ISBN 978-0-9979888-0-2

For Mom

Alexanne Bourdas Clarke

(July 5, 1941 – November 30, 2014)

AVAILABLE AS AN AUDIOBOOK

Chapter 1

A RUDE AWAKENING

"Mama," I yelled, rising up frantically in the bed, heart pounding in my chest. The dream was way too real. Mama was asking me to turn the TV on so she could watch QVC and the harder I tried to get to the TV to do so the further away it drifted until the wall just swallowed the TV leaving nothing but white space.

I had this foreboding feeling that something very bad was about to happen. And then it dawned on me. I had totally missed the QVC hour featuring Greek jewelry that I needed to watch to order Mama's Christmas present.

The phone rang. *Who is calling at this ungodly hour of the night?* I thought. *Geez, it's nearly…what?! 10 am. How in the world did I oversleep, missing my daily ritual of running at 6 am on the beach?* I was out of kilter in a bad way. The phone rang again.

"Yello."

"Hackett, it's your Dad."

"Hey, Dad. Happy Thanksgiving. I was meaning to give you a call." I rolled my eyes knowing full well that calling Dad on turkey day was low priority on my to do list.

"I'm calling about your Mama. You need to come on up and see her. The doctor is not expecting her to live much longer. And we're talking mere days, Hackett."

My heart sank. It was karma. I knew I should've watched QVC. I yelled out to my wife, Joelle. "Honey, did you DVR the QVC show last night?"

"Oh, let me think. No dear," Joelle hollered back with a healthy dose of sarcasm.

I returned the phone to my ear and continued, "Dad, how in Zeus' name did Mama's health deteriorate so quickly? I thought she still had nearly six months."

"I don't know what to tell you Hackett except that the inept doctor is a quack if you ask me. I never liked the man. He's as arrogant as he is incompetent."

Geez, I thought to myself. Dad is still hung up on his past hang ups with Mama's doctor. She swears by him and Dad swears about him. I could detect his mounting hostility so the last thing I wanted to do was say something to agitate him any more than he already was.

"Ok. I'll gather Joelle and the kids and we will be there by 8 pm. What are you doing for Thanksgiving?"

"I'm heading to your brother's house. Burt and Sonja have invited me over to spend Thanksgiving with their family. Your sister Lucinda and Phinn were also invited."

"Ok. Well try to enjoy your time. We've got to pack and then we'll hit the road to go see Mama." I hung up and couldn't help but think, *Good luck with Lucinda showing up with how she feels about Burt and Sonja. That's a disaster waiting to happen.*

My thoughts turned to Mama lying in a hospice room. Such an undignified way to go for such a dignified woman. Broke my heart to think about her in such a debilitating state. I remembered fondly saying to Mama on more occasions than one, "Dad's so mean he'll outlive us all. But I sure hope you outlive the old, grumpy badger." I hate it when I'm always right.

Oh, the good times that Mama and I shared. We were besties in every sense of the word. We leaned on each other and always enjoyed a good laugh. Just isn't fair how Death goes about selecting the pick of the crop. Of all people in this dastardly family, Death chose a dalliance with Mama.

It was just all so irksome. I so want to put a boot where the sun doesn't shine while giving Death a piece of my mind. My gut told me he wouldn't listen especially with a less than hospitable boot shoved up his backside. And I trust my gut for more than just processing food, let me tell you. Never mind about that but if there was a way to foil Death's plans with Mama I would try to find a way, that's for sure.

Chapter 2

ROAD TRIP

We had about a seven hour road trip ahead of us up to old Conundrum County not too far from the outer banks of North Carolina. Our kids: Louie, Allie, Kiwi, and Bixie were all crammed in our Dodge Ram Quad-Cab truck. The mobile gaming devices were fully charged and already burning up data usage. It's a wonder how parents made it through the Dark Ages without such mind-numbing devices to distract kids and proffer parents a much needed reprieve from little scalawags.

All thoughts both spoken and unspoken soon turned to ya-ya (Greek for Grandmother). "What's wrong with ya-ya?" Louie asked as he prepped to play a space game, obviously more excited about saving earth from aliens than ya-ya from an imminent rendezvous with the kiss of Death.

Explaining death and dying to a five year old presented a challenge because I certainly didn't want to say anything that could adversely impact his psychological well-being but on the other hand I didn't want to mislead him either so I chose the most prudent course of action afforded me under the circumstances.

"Ya-ya's gonna die son. The old black codger Death himself is rattling his chains and heading her way even now as we speak. The dark chariot has left the stable and we need to get there before he arrives."

Louie suddenly became wide-eyed as he looked up wearing a startled expression. His space ship warning systems on the game began repeating, "Alert! Alert! Approaching asteroid. Take evasive maneuvers." I could tell he was trying to get a grip on his little internal world as it began to spin out of control like the little spaceship that was zipping across his screen abruptly crashing into an asteroid. He was trying to process and shut down at the same time. It really was a psychological phenomenon to behold.

"It's ok, little bud. Ya-ya is getting ready to go to the Great Spirits. She will mount a great white Stallion and gallop off into a world of never-ending gaming and rivers flowing with crushed ice and Coca-Cola. She will walk among cotton candy trees and pick flowers made of taffy and bushes with Skittle berries growing all over them. The birds flying overhead will poop droppings of white chocolate. It's an amazing place where she's going."

"Can I go with ya-ya?" Louie asked excitedly.

Ok, maybe I over did it just a little. But wow! How quickly

Louie went from a fear of ya-ya dying to elation for where ya-ya was going. Basically in his mind, ya-ya's death was a necessary stepping-stone to get to candy heaven. *Whatever works for you,* I mused to myself.

"No, Louie. Ya-ya needs some time to ready her new home and do some happy place cleaning before she will be ready for any of us to come visit."

"How long does she need to clean?"

"At least another hundred years knowing your ya-ya. She needs some happy alone time but right now she is still with us although her mind has already gone to that happy place."

"Well how can my mind go to that happy place too?" Louie asked developing a level of interest I never anticipated.

"Dear God son, ya-ya is about to die and she is hiding the heck away from Death and his scariness. You don't want to go to that happy place until you hear Death's chains begin to rattle. Now play your game and pray to God that you don't hear any rattling for years to come!"

Louie dropped his eyes to the gaming screen and quickly immersed himself once again in his world of spaceships and hurtling asteroids. But at least the pressing questions stopped, for now.

Chapter 3

PASSING GAS

Oh, how the miles seemed to drag on for nearly an eternity. It's as if every blessed tree along the interstate was singing a lullaby as I fought to stay alert beneath a sleepy blue dome. I was really craving a few extra hours of sleep to energize my senses so I asked Joelle for one of those five hour energy drinks. She just said, "Uh huh." And kept reading her book swatting my request aside like an annoying fly. *Amazing,* I thought. Thoughts of Mama would have to suffice.

I really needed Mama to cease her mad dash toward Death's luring arms. The thought of Mama slipping from this world just didn't sit well with my reality. I was starting to experience heart palpitations at the thought of her seesawing with Death in a sick kind of romantic, playground affair.

I bet a couple Little Debbie Swiss Rolls would give Mama the strength she needed to resist Death's advances. My meandering thoughts were getting more active here of late, flitting across my mind like a wandering butterfly. I took it as a sign.

"Joelle, call the Hospice Care Center and see if they can get Mama a Swiss Roll. And make sure it's the Little Debbie brand. It's her favorite."

"Hackett, your Mama hasn't been eating solids for weeks now. Everything has been via IV," Joelle replied looking at me from the backseat like I had been living on another planet.

"Well, have you ever thought that maybe Mama just got dang tired of eating sterile foods and wants to get her yummy on again."

I turned the music on to drown out Joelle's response. Sometimes, it's just best to curtail the mooing to make one's point. "Your Mama don't dance and your Daddy don't rock and roll…" And then I begin to think of Mama and Dad's experiences with church life.

Dear God, I thought. Therein was always the problem with those two. If Dad would've gotten over his pastoral hang ups with church house politics then maybe he would've cut footloose with Mama and us kids more often.

Behind every fire and brimstone preacher is a hornet's nest of a church. Dad would always come home ready to strike like a viper. But we all knew how to scurry in a hurry. Didn't always escape though but I certainly learned the lay of a home in quick fashion as we moved quite a bit. Church folks are fickle. For a God who supposedly is the same yesterday, today, and forever; his groupies are about as schizophrenic as they come.

"Will you turn that down," Bixie said sitting over on the passenger side. Her words disrupted the random thoughts that I'm often fond of having. It's my only form of escape from the madness of it all.

"Are you serious?" I asked. "You know for a fifteen year old, you act like a granny. Asking me to turn down my tunes is like asking a frog not to swim in a pond, or a horse from running in a meadow, or asking me not to pay another dime for anything you will ever want again. There are some things you just don't ask."

Bixie just gave me her typical response, "Whatever?!"

The problem with this generation of upstarts is that they have been pandered to for far too long. Not me, never. I'm all about instilling respect and appreciation for all things parental. Like zipping it when Dad's playing his tunes unless you're singing along.

And then I heard a pop and caught a whiff of rotten eggs. *Geez*, I thought to myself. I must have just passed a chemical mill. I glanced over at Bixie who was wearing a big old grin on her face while vibing to tunes with earplugs stuck in her ears.

"Hey, stinky butt. You want to role that window down

over there?"

And then there was another pop. Bixie immediately spoke up as the truck swerved, "That wasn't me!"

Chapter 4

BLOWOUT ON THE ROAD

My life passed before my eyes as our Dodge Ram began to fish tail on Interstate 95 as "Grandma Got Run Over by a Reindeer" began playing. "Don't hit ya-ya," Louie belted out from the backseat.

It was pandemonium. All I could think to do at the time was just become one with the crazed atmosphere of emotional distress being displayed by a bunch of screaming banshees. "Hold your stink everybody, we're going to roll!"

And then as if from some angelic force of divine intervention everything seemed to just go into slow motion until the truck came to a stop off the interstate. A serene peace came over me as the dawn of realization washed over me rather quickly.

"Wait," I hollered as I jumped out of the truck looking for any sign of the angel of mercy. "Can you change the tire also?" So much for an actual divine specter. I turned and there was Louie chasing Allie and Kiwi around the truck trying to slap their butts. *This is not happening*, I thought. Oh, but it was and it was only getting started.

Suddenly memories of previous opportunities to buy tools necessary for just such an occasion began flooding my mind, like the time I was standing in an auto shop looking at a tire changing kit that included a shiny lug wrench and nut loosening lubricant and a sweet battery powered truck lift. I remembered thinking at the time, *Yeah right. Should call this place auto fear, a conspiracy of business minds seeking to prey on consumer anxiety.* Not me, I wasn't going to pay $29.95 for that kit. Funny how circumstances can change perspectives.

All I had was a lug wrench and a pathetic jack that looked like it was designed more for a Ford Pinto than a Dodge Ram truck. "This is not happening to me," I crooned softly as if trying to calm myself by suppressing the volcanic like emotions that were welling up inside of me. The only rational thought going through my mind at the time was, *I'm sorry Mama. I should've never traded the Acura. Oh, how Mama loved that Acura with those leather seats.*

"Hackett, you going to get this tire changed or just stand there like a jack ass on the road side looking like you don't know what the heck you're doing?" Joelle thundered in my ear. "Christ's sake," she continued not missing a beat, "it's like I married a nimwit who can't figure out a nut from a bolt. If you want to get to your Mama before she mounts the eternal chariot then you better get to wrenching and a changing."

Joelle had a way of motivating me. Morale began to sink quickly. I knew it was time to reach deep down and call forth some of that old time religion that always sweetened things between us. "How's about you go pray and smack talk God a bit, cause if you ain't gonna help me jack off this tire then maybe your services are better utilized elsewhere. Like maybe with Louie over there who is sticking his butt up in the air to everybody driving by."

"Dear Lord. Louie get back in that truck right now!" Joelle yelled and off she went.

Well Mama, Louie is certainly on his way to becoming President of the United States one day just like you said. He sure does know how to draw attention. I'll give him that, I thought while loosening a nut.

I gave myself to the task at hand and after being immersed in sweat, dirt, grease, and grime, the spare was in place and the Dodge fit for the road again. I just hoped that the remainder of the trip would prove uneventful. My gut told me that was wishful thinking. And it was.

Chapter 5

HUNGER PAINS

We were just riding along making good time and it suddenly dawned on me that we never ate lunch before we left. "Hey Dad?" Kiwi chirped.

"Yes, Kiwi. What you got stirring under the hood?"

"We never ate lunch."

She is such a chip off the old block! I thought proudly to myself.

"You know Kiwi, I was thinking that very thing."

"Well, can we stop and get something to eat?"

"Yeah Dad. Can we stop and get something to eat? Allie chimed in between thumb sucks.

Things were suddenly beginning to spin out of control. What seemed to be a bonding moment was now beginning to feel like an invasion of my parenthood. I didn't want to risk losing control of the situation so I thought it best to just take the bull by the horns and remedy the situation.

"Ok. Joelle, how about you? Did I hear a growl in the bowel?"

"That would be the gas I just passed. Now, find a place to

eat and be quick about it."

I knew when Joelle lost her patience that time was not on my side. But I also liked to live on the edge when it came to our relationship. It's what had kept our marriage interesting especially with a twenty-four year old, a fifteen year old, a nine year old, a seven year old, a five year old and our little Chihuahua named Queen Bean.

Oh, how I love our lil' Queen Bean. She's just so darn cute and expressive. Anytime Joelle would start running her trap, I would just look at the bean and start howling. Queenie can go from a yip yip to a full throttle howl that can rival that of any howling wolf. And her howl can really be quite angelic especially when Joelle starts a flappin' and a snappin'.

Oh geez, I thought anxiously as I hit the brakes and swerved over off the road. In the rush to get on the road, I had totally forgotten about Queen Bean. "Joelle, we've got to turn around. We left Queen Bean back at the house."

"Already taken care of her," Joelle said nonchalantly. "Betty Lou is looking in on her while we're gone. You just get us to an eatery. These kids are famished."

"I'm on it, woman," I replied. "Lighten up back there. Didn't you bring a couple books? Go chase a thought around."

"Hackett, you know your Mama loved Cracker Barrel."

Joelle had a way of redirecting and deflecting any of my

shenanigans. She had her own system of synchronization worked out which kept us both gelling like two peas in a pod. But more often than not it felt as if we were like cabbage and watermelon from two different patches.

Thank God for my survival skills. I learned early on in our marriage, to go along to get along, to avoid being miserable for long. Mama was adept in modeling such behavior when dealing with Dad's quirky behavior and stubborn mindset. He was a jerk. Still is. *Get a grip Hackett,* I thought to myself. *Just focus on Joelle and not on your Dad. She is the lesser of two evils.*

"You're right honey, bunny. Mama loved Cracker Barrel. And we're going to find us one before the sun dips down." I was starting to feel confident and in control again. It was just a feeling I got from time to time. That's what thoughts of Mama would do to me. Especially anytime I would think of Mama and Cracker Barrel together. The two are so empowering.

Chapter 6

CRACKER BARREL

I have to admit, it can really be frustrating looking for a Cracker Barrel when you need one. Why is it that anytime you actually want something it seems so elusive? Almost like it never existed. This happens to me quite frequently. At times I wonder if I'm the only one that feels this way. But then I see Louie run around every morning before school looking for his shoes, Allie her socks, Kiwi her hair brush, Bixie her back pack, and Queen Bean her greenie. It's probably genetic.

And there it was. "Great Balls of Fire", I hooted. Spiked high up on a billboard was the Cracker Barrel sign greeting us happy travelers like the first rays of the sun kissing the ocean as it ascends in radiant splendor above the grand watery horizon.

"Cracker Barrel!" I cried out.

"Whoomp! There it is!" Louie bellowed.

I could feel Mama's energy like a palpable get-up-and-go kind of energy. All kinds of emotional triggers were being pushed now that I had Mama stuck in my head with the

Cracker Barrel sign in actual view. I was being drawn into some kind of mystical vortex that gave me a strange otherworldly sensation. It felt good so I just went with it.

I leaned over and said to Bixie, "Hey, did you feel that sunshine?"

She just looked at me as if I was daft. "Umm, no!" Bixie seemed to have lost her fondness for being Daddy's girl like she used to be so proud of back in middle school.

What is up with the tweens? I mean, it's like they are the paragons of smarts and parents are embarrassingly stupid. As if we are cuckoo ca pooh. I never really get em'.

It really is an adolescent phenomenon to behold when the DNA deafness kicks in and you go from being celebrity to being "wouldn't wanna be ya". I was learning to cope and treating the whole psychological ordeal as an experiment in hormones. I am highly confident that I was never so imbecilic in my youthful days or ways.

I tried a more tacit response and just gave her that, "I'm on to you," look with a wry grin breaking across my beatific face. She wasn't eating what I was trying to put on her plate. It just became a silly standoff off with optical weirdness between us until a couple of car horns startled my tractor beam-like pull on her witchy eyes.

"Hackett, watch where the heck you are driving. Christ's sake you're gonna get us all killed," Joelle screamed out.

I quickly swerved and made good time peeling off across the grassy off-ramp and onto the exit to Cracker Barrel. "Now that was intense," I said, brushing off the danger of the moment.

"Yeah, Dad that was intense," Louie reeled off in flappable excitement.

"Thanks shishle," I said, looking back at him with a grin. Shishle is a word I created especially for Louie. It means, "Bestest bud in the whole wide world." And that we are. At least until he hits middle school.

And there it was just off to the right of the traffic light, we were within eyesight of the Cracker Barrel promise land. The air was nearly electric now with Mama-like energy. I knew I was channeling her oomph for the Barrel.

I couldn't wait any longer so I cut in front of a punch buggy and took a sharp right at the red light and flipped my hand up in a "what did I do" way at the honking beetle driver while whipping the Dodge over and into the traffic lane.

"You might want to read your traffic signs," Bixie said caustically.

"What you mean?" I retorted. "Right on red unless you're sitting next to Fred."

"Umm, the 'No Right Turn on Red' sign states differently."

It was too late. I was already committed. Besides,

Starship's song, *Nothing's Gonna Stop Us Now*, was playing. It was a sign.

Chapter 7

ROCKIN' AT THE BARREL

Nothing like the exhilarating feeling that comes over you when getting out of your vehicle after a long drive. And then badda bing, badda boom. Geez, what are the chances that we would open all four of our truck doors at the same time hitting the vehicles right next to us. More like badda dint, badda move.

So I told everyone to get back in and fortunately there was an open parking space directly behind us. I hate it when cars park without any thought as to the remote possibility of a Dodge Ram truck coming along and parking next to them. It's like inviting unwanted contact. Maybe that's what auto insurance was created for. Hopefully both cars have insurance. I do but keep it a private matter.

We all clamored out of the truck a little more cautiously and stealthily so as not to draw unwanted attention. I bent down and looked over at Kiwi and pointed two fingers at my eyes and then to her signaling for her to cross the parking lot. She knew from our countless hours of playtime at home exactly what I was communicating. She signaled back in similar fashion. *Daddy's girl*, I thought to myself with a beaming grin breaking across my face.

I looked over at Bixie and did the same, she just gave me her typical "whatever" expression and broke our cover as she brazenly walked on across the parking lot. Allie just put her thumb in her mouth and twirled her hair. Her signals confused Louie. He took off running across the parking lot in a mad sprint for the front door. I guess he thought Allie's thumb sucking signal was a green light for him to go use the restroom as speedily as possible.

I cast a quick glance behind me to Joelle and she returned mine with a glare that inspired dread as if I were bending down next to a corpse in a dark catacomb beneath the Vatican. A chilling sensation swept down my spine but I quickly brushed it off. This was not a time to be given to fear. So, I just pulled down on my ear and gave her a wink. She slapped her butt and then gave me a swift kick. I got up and hurriedly began walking.

Reaching the front entry area to the Cracker Barrel, our eyes were greeted by a vast assembly of rockers that simply looked inviting. Yes, we had been sitting for a long time but these were not just any ordinary rockers. These were Barrel rockers. If you've never experienced a Barrel rocker, you absolutely must put it on your bucket list. Oh, the tantalizing sensations that wash over your body when sitting in a Barrel rocker.

Bixie wasn't having any of it. She just went on inside to peruse the grand display of goods and wares for sale. The rest of us went butts down on a rocker of our choice and began to rock as sweet emotion claimed us. Ain't nobody, no how, can make a rocker better than the Barrel. It's like they use some kind of magical pixie dust so that when you sit on one you're swept away to a neverland of ecstasy and wonder.

I was starting to doze when Joelle hollered from down at the far end of the porch. "Hey, Hackett. You gonna come inside and join us for some vittles or just stay out here and rock it till you hock it?"

Joelle knew me well. I would make a great Barrel rocker salesman. My idea of a dream job actually. I would take the Barrel's entire rocking chair sales to a whole new level by training a sales force of professionals with a consulting tagline of: Pitch it! Rock it! Sell it!

Time was up. I jumped up and scuttled over to the front door and walked in with Joelle. She slapped me on the butt as I stepped across the threshold. It was her way of being frisky. I gave her a little wag as I strutted on by. She just glared at me. Another expression of affection.

Chapter 8

NEAR DEATH EXPERIENCE

I couldn't help but recall a memory of when Mama and Dad had left the hospital after Allie's birth to go eat at a Cracker Barrel. What an adventure that turned out to be. Dad was driving slowly as he typically does when driving along the lazy roads of Conundrum County without giving much thought to the fact that he was driving on Interstate 40; a veritable test of mental toughness and survival instincts. It's a survival of the fittest where if you're not fit you get hit. Well that was exactly what happened to Dad.

Driving along with the buzz of interstate traffic, Dad began to get nervous. He had found himself in the far left lane along a stretch of interstate that amazingly opened up to multiple lanes of madness causing his anxiety to kick into overdrive. As one accustomed to driving among serene cow pastures and quaint farm lands he found himself on the highway to hell. Dad's old clicker began clicking so rapidly that Mama thought she actually heard his cold, beating heart from the passenger's side.

"Dear God, Mama!"

Now Mama didn't know if he was crying out to his Mama or was crying out to her. But he was crying out to somebody of that she was sure. He would often call her Mama when he got real worked up and boy could Dad get worked up. At times, frightfully so.

"It's a hornet's nest out here," Dad spat. The traffic was buzzing along and around them as if they were the hive attracting all the honey bees. Dad's worst nightmare was unfolding at a bullet's pace. He only hoped that he could make it safely over to the slow lane before his heart or something worse came out of his chest. He took a quick glance in the rearview and went for it.

Mama recalled that at the moment he began to veer right, *Jesus Christ Superstar* (Jerome Pradon, Choir) began playing on the car stereo as everything suddenly went into slow motion. Mama remembered yelling, "Theodore watch out for…" But it was too late.

Turning directly into the path of a car, Dad's red Prius was like a red waving flag to a raging Spanish bull looking for something to impale. And sure enough that is just what happened. Dad was clipped in the right back end as he cut over and the red Prius and the interstate became like a circling merry-go-round with a variety of cars and trucks spinning by.

Several spins later and one hell of a scare, Dad and Mama found themselves still upright and safely on the far side of the interstate just out of reach of the oncoming traffic. Mama thought Dad was going to check out then and there. Her hopes were high but Dad quickly pulled out of his heightened state of anxiety. No chance he was checking out anytime soon.

They never made it to the Cracker Barrel that day but Mama was still grateful for the thrillfest of an experience. Any excitement to be had outside of Conundrum County was a welcomed relief for Mama. She always loved a good rollercoaster but that thrill ride with Dad along I-40 was a tale that only got better with the telling.

The life-threatening experience caused Dad to appreciate even more the safety, serenity, and sanity of his home among an acre of land in old Conundrum County. Mama wanted more, yearned for more, reached for more. But she knew that the accident on I-40 would only serve to deepen the bond between Dad and old Conundrum. And it did. Mama had a sixth sense that was always spot on. She would often say, "I hate it when I'm right about your Dad." She knew him all too well.

Chapter 9

SOUL RAIDERS

The fire within the fireplace blazed next to us in the Barrel as we all sat around a large round table. Louie was bending over and sticking his butt in the air and shaking it drawing unwanted attention. "Louie," Joelle snapped. "Get back in your chair, right this instant."

My cell phone went off distracting me from the embarrassment of the moment. "Yello."

"Hey Dad. What you guys up to?"

It was Jett, our twenty-four year old son who was stationed in Hawaii by the Air Force and currently visiting with a friend in Virginia. Now Jett and Mama were super close. They both loved Elvis, Mama's great love. Jett used to sweet talk Mama into letting him keep that old hound dog with him on weekends almost like they were sharing custody rights. Jett experienced some great teen years with Elvis and always loved going to ya-ya's to run the fields with him.

"Jett, we're at a Cracker Barrel on our way to see your ya-ya. She's slipping quickly so it's literally a race against the clock to get to her in time. Where are you?"

"I'm actually on my way to see ya-ya as well. Granddad called and asked if I could keep an eye on Elvis over the next several days. I just picked the old scoundrel up. What you want me to do?"

"Go by and see your ya-ya. Report back as soon as possible. Let me know the latest. We should be there in a few hours. And watch yourself. If your Uncle Burt and his clan show up guard your mind and exercise restraint."

"Got it Dad. I don't pay a lot of attention to that pious bunch so don't worry."

"They will be in force and circling like vultures, so just keep your wits about you son. If they start going for Mama's soul do your best to avoid a knee jerk reaction. They mean well but trying to save a soul on the death bed for their religious tribe is like a terrorist trying to convert an infidel. It's paradise or bust."

"Don't worry Dad. I've got this. I'll call at first opportunity after seeing ya-ya. Besides, I've got Elvis riding shotgun. Love you."

"I love you too, son. And Jett – give Mama a kiss on the forehead for me. Just in case."

"Don't worry Dad. She's not going anywhere at least not until she has seen you. Of that I have no doubt."

Joelle had ordered a late lunch while I was talking to Jett.

She ordered my typical Cracker Barrel favorite: French toast, eggs scrambled with cheese, turkey sausage, and OJ. Breakfast for early dinner is my kind of eating. It was delicious and soul-stirringly good.

As I was digging in, I looked over at Kiwi trying to play that cursed triangle thingy and get it to just one tee standing. "How you faring over there smarty smarts?" I asked.

"Got it down to four, Daddy."

"So what does that make you, a smart ignoramus?" I asked, smiling with egg on my face.

"Yep. I sure am!" She replied, beaming proudly.

Got to love her optimistic, winning attitude. Can't keep a good girl down. A daddy's girl if there ever was one. "You keep at it sweetsie and you'll be the master of the triangle thingy with a star on Cracker Barrel's Walk of Fame."

"Cracker Barrel doesn't have a Walk of Fame," Bixie said with a know-it-all look on her face.

"Well, maybe Kiwi will become the catalyst for the first star," I said while opening my mouth nice and wide to reveal a colorful array of mixed foods.

"Gross Dad. You're so not right," Bixie said turning her face away trying to avoid public embarrassment.

"Well let me pour you a tall glass of get over it," I replied before washing the fuss down with a big old gulp of Cracker Barrel's finest drinking water fresh out of the tap.

CHAPTER 10

ON THE ROAD AGAIN

We all loaded back into the Dodge Ram and hit the road for the final leg of our journey. I could tell everyone felt refreshed and ready for me to crank up the tunes. I mean what would a road trip be without tunes? So I put on one of my favorites, *Lay Down Sally* by Eric Clapton.

Eric didn't even make it to the first chorus line before the disruption of a classic began. First, it was Louie. "Dad, why does he keeping telling Sally to lay down?"

And then Bixie had to offer her two cents. "Because he needs to get a life."

Joelle couldn't leave well enough alone and tossed her hat into the arena, "Hackett, do you always have to play oldies. Get with the times and play something current and fresh."

I couldn't let her words stand. "You got to be kidding me? What is it with you and your lack of appreciation and disdain for music over a week old? Just because something is an oldie doesn't mean it's a moldy. How about that church you go to every week called *New Thing*, but they preach out of that old thing don't they?"

"And what old thing might that be?" Joelle said rolling her eyes.

"The Bible, woman. Book nearly two thousand years old. That old thing. Never tire of hearing those old tunes do you?"

"Don't you bring church into this. You do it every time disagreements arise. You may have had your fallen out with the church but I don't carry any ill will toward God's people."

"Kiwi, reach over there in the glove compartment and get that glue stick out and hand it to your Mama so she can put some on her lips." Kiwi started to reach over but then realized what I was asking and thought better of it. She glanced back wearing a, "Seriously?" expression on her face. I just smiled and winked.

I had to give it to Joelle, she knew me well. But I'm of the philosophy, "If the shoe fits wear it." But she and I differ over church matters. I know how that sausage is made, served, and dished out every week. And I didn't have a hankering to eating any of it.

Growing up within the sound of chapel bells and watching church politics suck the life out of Dad was enough convincing for me. Dear God, it had become glaringly obvious that the church mice were more worried about who moved their cheese than if the cheese was even worth eating in the first place. I had become convinced that Jesus meant what he said to the religious mice back in the day saying something to the effect that the Temple was desolate and nothing but a ghost town. Told them he was out of there or something to that effect. *The Message* version of the Bible got it right in Matthew 23:38-39. I merely followed his lead and smartly cut bait and moved on from organized religion as well.

I lost count how many times that Joelle and I had gone round and round like a merry-go-round over church and religion. I'm all for God and spirituality but when you throw organized religion into the mix, it's like adding vinegar to milk and honey. Vinegar is good for collards and pouring on urine stains. Other than that, I don't have much use for vinegar and organized religion and I'm of the mindset that the good Lord above doesn't either. He loves the people but not too keen on the religion.

But unfortunately to keep the peace, I learned to use honey with Joelle and at times generously so. I knew there was wisdom in tip toeing discreetly around the issue of church and religion. But now wasn't the time for honey. So I gave Joelle a healthy dousing of vinegar and said, "Woman, God is no more a church goer than Bixie over there is a virgin."

Dear God, you would've thought the end of days was

suddenly upon us by the soul-blistering verbal assault from yours truly. I leaned over and asked Louie, "We there yet?"

Chapter 11

JETT

Making good time and only a few hours out from the Hospice Care Center, my cell phone rang. Answering I said, "Yello."

"Dad, this is Jett."

"Go ahead, Jett."

"I'm sitting on Vulture's Row." Jett was using military speak for the viewing gallery on an aircraft carrier for observing flight operations. He was outside Mama's hospice room watching the nurses and doctors treat patients.

"What you observing on Vulture's Row?"

"Oh Lord," Bixie said rolling her eyes while looking out the passenger window. "You both need to so grow up."

"What was that?" Jett asked.

"It's nothing. Just a bit of wind smack," I said, looking over at Bixie who just curled her lips up in a snarl scrunching her eyebrows. I thought maybe she was going to sneeze so I pointed to the glove compartment. "Should be some tissue in there."

Bixie just rolled her eyes again saying her typical, "Whatever."

"You know, you really need to expand your vocabulary beyond 'whatever', 'really', and 'Oh Lord'. And one of these days those eyes are going to roll out of the sockets and onto your lap."

"Dad, is that Bixie?"

"Yup. Just a chirpin' away. Look, tell the nurse to let you in the hospice room."

"It's ok Dad. I made it in there for a few minutes before the nurse came in."

"How is Mama doing?"

"She is not doing well. Didn't say anything. Burt and his crew showed up so I stepped out of the room. He was telling everybody to gather around ya-ya for pictures. And get this. He was telling everyone, 'this might be the last time to get a chance to be in a picture with ya-ya while she's alive.' Can you believe that?"

"So typical of Burt. Did he go for the save?"

"I don't know Dad. I had to walk out. I can't take but so much of their pious bull malarkey."

"Ok. You've done good Jett. We should be there in a couple of hours. Let them know at the nurses station it will be after hours when we arrive. You going to be around?"

"No. I'm heading over to Jade's. Let me know if anything

changes with ya-ya. She looks like she's starting to see a light and not the one coming from inside the room."

I hung up and all I could do was drive in silence. The dawn of realization was rising steadily in my mind's eye. It would only be a matter of time before one of the greatest spirits to have ever lived would depart this world. I tried to imagine what it would sound like. I mean, does a great spirit create a sonic boom upon departing the body? I sure as heck would if someone was in my hospice room trying to save my soul. Even if I weren't right with the Almighty, death is no time to be making enemies, especially with the Devil.

Melancholy began to settle over me like a pall over a coffin. It was dreadful to think of Mama checking out and leaving me behind to face life without her in it. Mama was such a sweet, caring soul. I could always call her when I needed to hear a cheerful voice on the other end.

Dad, on the contrary, was a tongue full of lemon. The church contributed considerably to the tartness that resided in him. I could certainly relate to his often dour moods. Heck, I never even started drinking spirits until I got involved in youth ministry. And by that point, my tolerance for church life had reached critical mass. After eighteen intolerable years growing up alongside sanctimonious churchians, I left the hive of hypocritical hellions behind and took the spirits with me.

And then it hit me. I sure hoped Mama had settled her affairs and made those as clear to Dad as she had to me. A bad feeling came over me like gnats on a midsummer's day. What had been done was done. And what hadn't been done well, was too late now. I could only hope.

Chapter 12

THE LAST SUPPER

We arrived at the Hospice Care Center where Mama had been transferred from the hospital. We all crawled out of the truck knowing that this was it. I walked toward the front doors with only thoughts of Mama. I couldn't believe she was about to depart this life and take her place with the Great Spirits.

It was all I could do to fight back an upwelling of grief ready to burst forth like mighty rushing waters released from a dam. Nothing can prepare you for the day you are to say your final good bye to your Mama. Well this was my day and as I walked up the sidewalk toward the Hospice Care Center I felt like a dead son walking. Facing the stark reality that Mama was leaving and not coming back, it became the longest walk of my life. Nothing can prepare you for it. I tried to think feel good thoughts about Santa and his reindeer but even that didn't help.

The nurse greeted us at the front door with a smile and led us back to where Mama was being kept comfortable in a hospice room. As we walked in, I was pleasantly surprised locking eyes with Mama. It was like beholding an angel robed in bed sheets. Mama was chillaxin' in her own dignified way.

I was never more proud of my Mama than in that moment. She couldn't speak. I could tell she was fighting back the meds which were steadily being fed to her body through an IV drip. Her eyelids kept drooping but she was aware that we were all gathered around. I was simply in awe and wonder at how someone could be so close to crossing over to the other side and yet, command her own mortality. She possessed a resolve that even Death himself respected, "Not yet. Not yet."

It was as if we were gathered around a saint about to leave this world. We were on holy ground. At least it was for me. It was our last supper with Mama IV drip style. But that was ok. Although we couldn't pass the bread and wine our cup of love flowed plentifully. My heart was filled with pride and love for Mama who had always been there for me throughout my life. I was just so thankful she was able to hang on so that I could see her one last time before the grand matriarch of our family departed this life. It was her moment to shine in our hearts and minds. And that she did!

We gathered around Mama as the kids took turns giving her loving embraces and butterfly kisses on her cheeks. Everyone then walked out of the room giving me a few moments alone time with Mama. I fought back the tears but couldn't contain myself any longer. I knew this was it and Mama did as well. Our eyes locked one last time before she gracefully and lovingly closed them. It would be our final moment together. I bent over and kissed her forehead and whispered how much I loved her. A weak smile creased across her face but her eyes remained closed. I waited and hoped they would open again but Mama was letting me know it was time for me to let go and leave.

When she didn't stir again, I knew it was her way of politely asking me to leave now and to leave her in peace. So I turned and walked away pausing at the door to take one final look back. "Good bye, Mama. I'll love you forever and then some." And those were the last words I spoke to Mama while she was alive.

I walked out of the room and down the hall where Joelle was waiting for the kids.

"You ok?" Joelle asked.

"Yeah, I'm ok."

"Wait here with the kids, I need to go use the restroom for a minute," Joelle said as she briskly walked back up the hallway taking a detour into Mama's room. Mama and Joelle were close. I knew it was as hard for Joelle to let go as it was for me. That was the kind of effect Mama had on those she loved. And that's what made her so special.

Chapter 13

CHURCH, GOD, AND ANIMALS

We arrived at our oceanfront hotel and carried our luggage inside. It was a pet friendly hotel with lots of dogs running loose. It was the only kind of hotel Mama would stay at when going on road trips. And this one was an oceanfront delight.

Mama loved animals. She spent most of her life as a veterinarian assistant saving and nurturing back to health many an animal. She taught us kids growing up that if there was a heaven animals would get in before people. And as such, we were to treat animals with the kind of dignity, love and respect the four-legged kind deserved. I took her literally.

A Greyhound walked over in a regal manner and upon approaching I immediately dropped to my knees assuming a posture of homage as a humble subject of the animal kingdom. He took a sniff of my backside and sort of casually walked on. Of course, before I could rise I heard someone say, "Oh God. No he didn't. Mom, I'll be outside." It was Bixie.

Before I could rise to my feet, I was pounced on by an

adorable, white poodle giving me generous amounts of wet kisses. Taking it as a high, holy sign I lovingly embraced the powder puff taking a lot of tongue on my face. It was a spiritual moment. Mama would've taken great delight in the whole affair.

Finally, after much licking and a few verbal yip yaps, I leaned over and sort of just hollered after Bixie, "Hey, come on cupcake. Show some love to the four-legged kind." She wasn't having any of it. I couldn't help but see a little bit of Mama in her. It wasn't that Bixie didn't like animals. To the contrary, she loved animals just like Mama and especially dogs. No, Bixie was just at that age where she wanted her world to be painted picture perfect and if anything smeared her canvas she just needed a little time to get the colors meshing once again. At least that is, until the next splotch from Dad's actions messed her picture perfect world up again.

Bixie like Mama would let you know in a heartbeat where she stood on a matter if she felt you needed to be told. I remember on one such occasion when Mama gave a piece of her mind to the leadership board at Dad's church. She didn't hold back when saying, "You know, after serving as a pastor's wife for nearly forty years, I'm practically a professing atheist." You could've heard the flutter of angel wings around that room. And of course, when Dad got home, he said what he was oft known to say to Mama, "Dear God Annabelle. Did you really have to go and speak your mind? Some thoughts are just best kept to one's self."

But Mama wasn't having any of it. She had zero tolerance for all the mean-spiritedness and backbiting within churches. And she made sure that I didn't follow in Dad's footsteps. She didn't have to worry about me. The last thing I wanted to do was be a preacher. I enjoyed drinking too much. Of course, I had a few close friends that belonged to the drinking churches who'd give attendees free shots of wine on certain Sundays.

No, I frankly got tired of all the moving around we had to do growing up. And most of it had to do with the fickle nature of the folks sitting in the pews. But Dad didn't have the gumption to stand up to the powers to be like Mama told him to do on more than one occasion. I still can hear her saying to him, "Theo, people only have as much power over you as you give em'. So the surest way to gain the upper hand is to disempower them. The pulpit in a stubborn church is better served splintered and doled out to a fire pit than trying to use it in a pointlessly rambling effort to speak sense to unreasonable and irrational souls. We can make a go of it back home in Charleston."

But Dad didn't listen. He was obstinate like that. No, Dad had to be faithful to his "Call", and felt it was for such stubborn and lost church folk who needed Jesus the most. *Whatever Dad*, I often thought to myself while hearing such spats between Mama and Dad over church affairs.

It all came to a head during my Junior year of high school, when I gave the bishop a piece of my mind. He came to preach at our church one Sunday, and after the service during a board meeting, he proceeded to announce that Dad was going to be moved. Well, I walked right into the closed meeting and told him, "You can shove that power trip you're on where the divine light don't shine. This wagon train ends here!"

I thought Dad was going to fall through the floor. But like Mama, I had had enough of organized religion. Don't get me wrong, there are some good-hearted folks in churches but they are few and far between. Like diamonds in the rough kind of folk. They're usually the quiet types because if they become vocal they will be dragged off at the behest of the local tribal chief and given the choice of either being blackballed or sing in the choir. And Dear God, have mercy on anyone that gets conscripted to sing in a church choir. Mama firmly believed and told Dad often that, "when Satan fell from Heaven he landed in the choir loft. And that silver-tongued Devil has been wailing in churches ever since."

No siree. Mama didn't have much love for the church during her years serving as a pastor's wife. And "SERVING" is how she felt. Like she was serving a prison sentence. Now don't misunderstand. Mama loves Jesus. She just never warmed nor took a liking to the church.

Mama didn't complain about her lot in life being married to a preacher and all. It's just that she wasn't in her right mind when she chose to do so. Mama reminded us kids on more than one occasion, "I was out of my mind when I met your father." And she was. She was a psychiatric patient when she first met Dad, who at the time, was working as a seminary intern on the psych ward. That was her story and she always stuck to it. And that is a tale for another time. And there will be. Another time.

I, more than anyone, understood why Mama gravitated to animals. They are kind, loving, affectionate, and loyal. We certainly didn't experience that from church folk. Mama felt more the love of God from the animal kind than she ever did from the religiously inclined, human kind. Mama said, "God got it right when he created the animals but then screwed up when he created the humans. And paradise went to hell in a handbasket soon thereafter."

I always found Mama's preaching more palatable than I ever did Dad's. I said more "Amen" from upstairs in my bedroom while listening to Mama go round and round with Dad over church matters than I ever did during worship service while listening to him drone on while frothing about at the mouth. Probably because I always fell asleep as the acolyte. But Mama's brand of truth was foolproof, you can believe that.

Chapter 14

ALL IS CALM, ALL IS BRIGHT

After checking into our adjoining hotel rooms overlooking the ocean we settled in for the night. Once the kids were tucked in and well on their way to dreamland, Joelle and I stepped out onto the balcony where our eyes were greeted by an enchanting starry night sky. Beautiful and auspicious, I had this innate sense that something special was in the works.

Among the canopy of luminous stars, one especially shone brightest, its luminescence twinkling causing goose bumps to break out along my neck and arms. A tingly sensation rifled down my spine causing me to physically shudder. Joelle looked at me with a start and said, "Hackett, the Devil got a hold of you or something?"

"No sugar love," I said, giving her a wink. "But if the Devil is up there flickering in the guise of that huge, shimmering star then he's certainly got my attention. Have you ever seen a more perfect evening sky? It's absolutely stunning." It made me feel all frisky inside.

A cold Atlantic breeze swept over us as we both continued

to gaze at the twinkling stars that seemed to dance among a black velvet backdrop. I reached over to take hold of Joelle's hand whereupon she popped the heck out of mine.

"What did you do that for?" I whimpered while quickly retrieving my throbbing paw.

"I thought it was a cockroach or spider crawling on me," Joelle cackled as her stomach began gyrating in laughter.

"You ain't right woman," I replied favoring my wounded paw.

"Hackett, you know I'm not into a lot of hand holding. When it comes time for you to hold me then by God you better do it as if your life depended on it. But right now, I don't want any hand holding. Just star gazing."

"Yes, dear," I said resolutely while gazing admiringly at the starry heavens. All was calm. All was bright. And then a haunting gloom swept over me as thoughts of Mama in that hospice room filled my mind once again.

"Joelle, I'm not sure how much longer Mama will be with us. When I told her I loved her and said good bye before I left, a feeling came over me that I would never see her again alive." My eyes misted over as I continued to gaze up at the mysterious heavens.

"Your Mama loves you Hackett. You've always been her favorite. Your brother Burt and sister Lucinda just never ascended to that special place in her heart like you did. I know this is hard on you but the love you and your Mama share is stronger than death itself."

Glancing over at Joelle with a smile I said, "Honey, you always know just what to say." She reached over gently placing her hand on mine. "And my love for you is of the same stock as your Mama's, my sweet, slice of watermelon."

That's my Joelle. The love of my life and my bright shining star. We certainly have our fair share of friction but it is always our steadfast love for each other that keeps us coming back for more. Mama and Dad were the same way. I couldn't recount all the times those two went at it but at the end of the day they were still on the side of love. Joelle and I share a love made of the same kind of grit. A love that at the end of the day is as calm as it is bright.

Chapter 15

ELVIS ON THE DOCKS

I couldn't sleep a wink. First it was the pillow. It was so soft that I felt as if I was laying my head flat on the mattress. There were only three pillows and of course I got the short end of the stick. Joelle pulled her usual blab it and grab it game she so often does when we stay at a hotel. The object to the game is, the first person to blab it, gets to grab it. So upon walking into the hotel room the first thing she does is startle the heck out of me by yelling, "Those two pillows are mine!"

"Good Lord, Joelle. You about gave me a heart attack." Then I tried to play the sympathy card. "It was such a long day behind the wheel and changing that tire along with the emotional end to the day has created a hankering for a couple soft pillows." Joelle just gave me a Bixie kind of look and said, "Talk to the hand because the face is on vacation."

"Whatever," I nonchalantly replied Bixie style. "You're heartless." But she was my panda bear so I gladly yielded to her more deserving comfort.

As I laid in the bed perfectly miserable, I couldn't help but ponder how a bag of soft marshmallows would be more preferable than the lousy thin pillow supporting my head. Over it, I got up and walked back out to the balcony and feasted my eyes on the beauty of the stars and moon shining down from above. While listening to the rhythmic sounds of the waves crashing on the shore, thoughts of Mama began drifting through my mind.

She had endured two years of dealing with the debilitating nature of Parkinson's disease which slowly deprived her of the quality of life she enjoyed during her years of physical vitality. Never complaining she took her deteriorating health in stride. Elvis, her beloved hound dog, was a great source of encouragement and inspiration for Mama even more so than Dad. I think he got a little jealous of Elvis at times but he would never admit it.

Mama and Elvis shared some fun times together, that's for sure. I'll never forget when we all went down to the docks along Shem's Creek which feeds into the Charleston Harbor. Well, Elvis got a hankering for some fish steaks and broke loose from the leash he resented having to wear when taken into town. Running down the boardwalk he came up rather fast behind a middle-aged couple leisurely strolling along enjoying their cones of ice cream. Spooked out of their wits they both just leapt off the boardwalk right into the creek. And then the folks sitting at the outdoor bar area of the

Creek Side Restaurant, started hootin' and a hollarin' which got Elvis all stirred up and baying at the top of his lungs. At that point, folks enjoying a few tall ones while taking in the sunset views over the harbor began howling along with Elvis egging him on.

Not missing a beat, Elvis left the crooning to the bar hoppers and kept running along until he just sort of went airborne off the dock and right onto a paddle board knocking a tourist right off and into the water. Elvis simply surfed right across the creek carried along by the momentum of his landing to the other side upon which time he leapt up and onto the dock where a fisherman was unloading the days catch. The fisherman was so amazed at Elvis' determination to get him a taste of some seafood that he handed him a nice size Speckled Sea Trout.

"That's my Elvis," Mama said cackling all the while. That was definitely a highlight we all enjoyed with Mama and Elvis. Looking out at the ocean enjoying the memory my thoughts soon turned dour once again. I began to see what appeared to be a very large ship out on the ocean that looked like the Titanic. It began to descend beneath the dark horizon almost as quickly as it appeared. Soon it vanished from view. My mind was starting to play tricks on me. I guess I was in the beginning stages of grief. Mama was my unsinkable Titanic and now the dark, watery grave was drawing her down within its dark abyss.

My disturbing thoughts were interrupted by the ring tone of my cell which began playing "Dixieland Delight" back in the hotel room. My heart sank. I glanced down at my watch and it was almost 2 am. I knew that a call this time of morning couldn't be a good thing. And it wasn't.

Chapter 16

THE CALL

Answering the phone with a calmness that bordered on emotional numbness, Dad's voice greeted me with his typical, "Hackett, it's your Dad."

For some odd reason he always began his calls with a reminder of who he was in relation to me as if I were suffering from dementia. It was so typical of our relationship, more professional than personal, all business and straight to the point. A succinct kind of father and son association. The kind every son dreams of having. Not.

"I know Dad. Did you think I forgot the sound of your voice?"

"What was that?"

"Nothing Dad. Whatcha doin' up before the Conundrum rooster crows?"

"I received a call from the hospice nurse. Your Mama died an hour ago. I would've called earlier but I got sidetracked. The nurse said she tried to call me and received no answer. I did answer but she hung up as I picked up the phone. So she called your brother Burt. So he ups and drives over to the Hospice Care Center like some kind of knight in shining armor. Of course, your Mama had already died before he got there."

My heart sank. I knew Mama's death was imminent but nothing prepares you for the actual reality. But where I was feeling sadness Dad seemed agitated. I got the sense from his spiteful tone that he found comfort and took consolation in the fact that Mama passed before Burt could get to the Hospice Care Center in time.

Clearly, Dad resented the nurse calling anyone but him. And he certainly didn't like that Burt had received the official death call and not him. It wasn't that Dad and Burt didn't have a close relationship because they did. But with Dad there were certain personal matters that you had better leave well enough alone or you would unleash the hounds of hell if you ran interference. And it sounded like Burt had unwittingly done just that.

"You think Mama was somehow aware that Burt was coming to pray for her soul and she decided to check out?" I couldn't restrain myself from taking advantage of the situation and getting Dad all riled up. Mama and I knew how to push Dad's buttons and at times we couldn't resist a prod or two for love of the sheer pleasure.

"Oh heck, you know Burt. Got to make a grand scene and

feel all important. Didn't have much to do with your Mama when she was alive but feigns his unwavering love during her passing."

Dad was some kind of bent out of shape by the way he was mouthing off about Burt. Their relationship was a comedy of errors with most of it revolving around that cursed stump of a root called evil, MONEY. And it most certainly was when it came to Burt and his incessant need for regular financial bailouts. Mama felt little compassion for Burt and his financial nonsense. She'd buck him and insist that Dad use the refining fire of tough love and tighten the purse strings.

Burt's faith must've been a perpetual frustration as the love of money was ever a thorn in his side. His "name it and claim it" faith simply wasn't strong enough to loosen God's purse strings. Finding little pampering from God, Burt looked to Dad to come through in answer to his desperate prayers for more money.

Burt was ever on the learning curve when it came to the green backs. He had a weakness for living beyond his means as if testing the limits of faith itself. I believe that Burt's financial woes were faith lessons that Jesus tried to teach him to no avail. Sort of like Jesus saying, "Burt, dude. Faith is not about showing you the money." And then Burt would be like, "But Jesus, dude. What cents would faith make then?"

Burt professed such great faith but Jesus would keep putting him in timeout with an empty wallet. Jesus simply refused to show him the money. So Burt looked to Dad to do what Jesus obviously wouldn't. And most of the time Dad would. Burt had a good thing going with Dad and he knew it.

Now, Mama resented the heck out of Dad always bailing Burt out of his financial messes. She'd let Burt have it. "The Devil's got a hold of your wallet boy. Stop chargin' and start changin'."

Oh my, how she would dish back Burt's pious talk and expose the error of his ways. Mama wouldn't put up with any religious mumbo jumbo. No siree. Not Mama. She wouldn't have any of it. But Dad would somehow smuggle the money to Burt anyway.

I just tried to stay out of Burt's religious vortex to avoid getting sucked up in his tornadic dogma that often kept Dad and Mama at odds with one another. I think Dad was just proud of Burt's going down the religious road like he did. Burt took religion to a whole new level with his own clan of soul raiders who could play a number on your mind and have you confessing to sins you never committed. A soul saved for Burt was like hitting a homerun. And that prophesying church he attended loved to hear about Burt's homeruns. I seriously doubt if Burt ever saved a soul in his life but he swears by all things holy that he has.

But Mama wasn't eating any of what Burt tried to put on her plate. She'd rather go and sup with the animals than partake from Burt and his clan's religious smorgasbord of nonsense. That's what I loved about Mama. She stuck to her guns and would draw em' without a moment's hesitation if she was caught in a standoff. Badda bing, badda boom. Such was Mama. But now more than ever, Mama was going to need me to draw her guns for her.

My thoughts suddenly turned to where Mama's remains would be buried or scattered for that matter. Heck, I didn't know if Mama had even made her wishes known to Dad although she had with me. But I was beginning to feel anxious that maybe she didn't ever think to have her last will and testament drawn up by an attorney.

My heart sank again. I knew that if Mama was to have any lasting peace beyond the grave, I needed to find out what Dad's intentions were regarding her remains. I didn't have to wait long to find out.

Chapter 17

AN INSPIRED PLAN

Feeling restless, I quietly snuck out not wanting to disturb Joelle and the kids. I needed some fresh, salt air to clear my mind. It's something I learned from Mama growing up. Often I'd find her out early walking the beach. It was one of her morning rituals. She would say, "Salt air opens the mind like Vick's vapor rub opens the sinuses."

I could feel Mama's spirit as I strolled along the beach enjoying the predawn morning. As I paused to behold the first light of dawn as the sun peaked over the Atlantic, I was reminded of what Mama said during one of our early morning walks. "Watching the sunrise is like being greeted by the magnificence of Heaven's brilliance." And it was. I smiled contentedly as dawn's early morning light first touched the Atlantic's horizon. It was like watching God masterfully put touches of paint on a canvas visually and audibly enhanced by the sounds of gulls crying and waves collapsing on the shore.

While strolling peacefully along captivated by the moment the sound of feet swiftly gaining traction through the sand moving in my direction caught my attention. I turned to see Elvis galloping along with ears flapping in the breeze, a sight for sore eyes.

"Come here boy," I said as Elvis eagerly leapt into my arms generously soaking my face with slobbery kisses. I gave him a few in return minus the slobber. "How'd you get out here, ole boy?" I looked up and saw Jett taking his shoes off back at the hotel boardwalk.

"Hey pops!" Jett hollered. Jogging over he came up and gave me a slap on the back. "How you holding up?" Jett said with a look of concern on his face.

"I already miss her."

"I hear you," Jett said simply. He and Mama were close so I knew it was his way of conveying succinctly, "I'm tracking with your emotions."

And then as if hearing the voice of Gabriel himself, I heard the most heavenly sound, "White tail buck deer munching on clovers, red tail hawk sittin' on a limb," and then I realized that my cell phone was ringing in my pocket. I pulled it out and Dad's number popped up on the screen. "It's Dad. Let me get this," I said, turning back toward the ocean.

"Yeah, Dad." I cut to the chase with a sinking feeling that the issue of how Mama would be laid to rest was the purpose behind Dad's call. And it was.

"Hackett. It's your Dad."

Geez, did he not just hear me call him Dad? I thought to myself.

"I need to speak you about your Mama's funeral. Well actually it will be a memorial service because I'm having your Mama cremated and buried in the Historic Conundrum County Cemetery." The matter-of-fact tone Dad used was his way of saying "this is the way it's going to be done, end of discussion." I needed to proceed with caution because the wrong word would set Dad off, sort of like stepping on a land mine.

"Ok. Were those Mama's wishes?" I knew full well what her wishes were but wanted to see if Dad had an inkling. Well, I had just stepped on a land mine.

"The decision what to do with your Mama's remains and where to bury her are mine alone to make," Dad said with growing hostility in his voice. "Your Mama didn't discuss her wishes with me regarding where she was to be buried." *Bull malarkey*, I thought to myself.

"I'm not going to bury her in Charleston. It is too far away. She will be buried here in the Historic Conundrum County Cemetery." Before I could counter he continued to tell me the plans for Mama's memorial service and burial, "The Bishop will preside and the Conundrum Church minister will assist. The memorial service will be in the chapel at the funeral home and then we will put your Mama's ashes inside a vault which will be buried in the ground."

Knowing better than to challenge him, I was caught in a bad spot with a sinking feeling in the pit of my stomach. I couldn't let this stand but risked alienating Dad, Burt, and Lucinda creating a family feud rivaling that of the Hatfield and McCoy's. But my first allegiance was to Mama whose spirit would never be free to enjoy her eternal rest if her remains were buried in old Historic Conundrum Country Cemetery. Nor would I be able to live with myself if I didn't take action to honor her request.

A vivid flashback of Mama jokingly saying to me, "Lord, if I go first your Dad will try and have me buried in the Historic Conundrum County Cemetery." And then she gave me as serious a look as I think she has ever given me before or sense in her lifetime when she sternly commanded, "Don't let him do it!"

My worst nightmare was becoming a reality as I was now faced with having to act quickly. But first I needed a plan.

"Ok, Dad," I said. "I've got to go and break the news to the family. I'll be in touch."

I hung up and glanced over at Jett who was down on bended knee next to Elvis both returning my gaze.

"So, what's the plan?" Jett asked. He knew me well.

"I'm not sure," I said, looking back toward the ocean. "But I'm in bit of a pickle. To honor Mama's wishes, I will alienate Dad. To honor Dad's wishes, I will alienate my heart. Always been the story of my life," I said, feeling more exacerbated by the moment. Elvis took off running distracting me from my thought as he high tailed it back to the boardwalk. *What is that crazy dog up to now?* I thought as my wheels were spinning pondering a possible way out of the present dilemma.

"Come here boy," Jett called out to Elvis. He ran back with his large, pendulant ears flopping up and down with a shoe in his mouth. He walked over to me, disregarding Jett. In his mouth was Jett's shoe. He dropped it at my feet and looked up at me with those doleful brown eyes of his. "That's not my shoe boy," I said, smiling down at him. "That's Jett's."

Bending down, I picked it up and tossed it over to Jett. Elvis leapt up and grabbed the shoe right out of Jett's hand. He carried and placed it once again at my feet. Jett laughed and said, "I think he's trying to tell you something."

"Yeah, like wear your shoes rather than mine. As if my shoes stink or something. Crazy dog," I said while patting him on the head.

"Well we do wear the same shoe size," Jett said with a chuckle.

For as long as I can remember, I've believed in animal intelligence and that they can think as strategically as humans.

It was just a theory I had. Some may consider me imbecilic but maybe I'm just naïve enough to believe that even old Elvis could come up with a splendid idea like the one that was forming in my mind of switching Mama's ashes; like switching out a pair of shoes.

And then it hit me as if a light suddenly went on. "Wait a minute. I've got an idea that just might work."

"What's that?" Jett asked, sensing the seriousness in my voice.

"We're going to switch Mama's ashes. And we're going to do it right up under Dad's obstinate nose," I said, feeling suddenly inspired and excited.

"Ok," Jett replied not totally sure if I had lost my marbles or not. "So, how and with what are you going to switch ya-ya's ashes?"

"I'm not sure but it will come to me. Always does." I gave Jett a slap on the back and said, "Come on, let's get the kids up."

I glanced down at Elvis and said, "What you think old boy? Brilliance in motion, don't you think?" He returned my gaze and then glanced over at Jett as if saying, "I resemble that remark."

CHAPTER 18

FIERCE DETERMINATION

My mind was racing with possible ways to switch Mama's ashes. The challenge moving forward was to create a foolproof plan that would have Dad thinking his will was being done on earth as he imagined it was in Heaven. But more importantly, to ensure that Mama's actual remains would be scattered upon her hometown soil of Charleston, the soil she considered most sacred in the whole wide world. Of one thing I was certain, come Hell or high water I was going to switch Mama's ashes.

My clan loaded up in the Dodge Ram and we headed over to visit with Dad. After nearly an hour we pulled up at Dad's home that sat on about an acre of land that backed up to the Conundrum swamp frequented by lots of deer and raccoons. The animals were the silver lining Mama found in living out in the boonies.

If not for the critters, I do believe Mama would've lost her sanity. She was a dignified woman and her values and tastes were considerably different than Dad's. And oh, how they often clashed. Never one to mince words, Mama was often the spark that lit his fuse resulting in fireworks of the kind you didn't want to watch when going off.

Dad had contrary opinions, tastes, and values much different than Mama. It was a wonder how they remained married for as long as they had. It was a brave and dangerous thing to speak one's mind around Dad. He could be extremely close minded and would as soon shoot a democrat before putting down a rattler. There was only one way in life and that was his way. It was probably why Dad tolerated Mama's love of Elvis Presley. He certainly loved the song Elvis made famous, *My Way*. That song summed Dad up perfectly.

We pulled up into the yard and Louie was first to get out by scrambling and crawling over me and jumping out the door. He was excited to be at Grandpa's. They had a special relationship. Funny how it works that way. My relationship with Dad was more like that of a Continental soldier to a British soldier during the Revolutionary War, more guarded than open. But Louie was Dad's patriot. He loved his Grandpa and Grandpa loved little Louie.

I walked up the broad steps leading to the front door. I knocked a few times before waiting for Dad to open. The wind howled through the surrounding woods giving me an eerie feeling that the spirits were unsettled. I heard Dad's footsteps inside approaching and then the door opened.

"Hey Hackett. Well hello little Louie." Wasting no time, Louie squeezed by me and wrapped his arms around his Grandpa. We all funneled inside and found a seat around the cozy den. Mama had pictures of family on the walls. And course, dispersed around the coffee table and counter spaces were souvenirs she had picked up on our trip to Greece together. Those were some good times we all shared among the Greek Isles.

Mama was a third generation Greek and a Spartan at heart. It was where she got her spunk and grit as well as her shine when a situation warranted a bright light. Dad would often get upset with Mama when she chose church socials to shine her light.

Mama was fiercely protective. She wasn't afraid to speak up if a loud mouth church bitty had the gumption to fire off at the lips about Dad or us kids. I remember on one occasion when this lady who was a busy body in the church acted on a fool-hearty impulse to ask my Mama, "Do you really think your boys need to be sleeping on the front pew during worship when they're serving as acolytes?" Mama replied in her typical matter-of-fact way, "Honey, you need to cut your own weeds." And of course, word would always reach Dad about the inappropriate way Mama spoke to someone at church. Dad would say, "Dear God Annabelle. Must you always speak what you're thinking?" But Mama would just reply, "Theo dear, when it doesn't fit I'm not wearing it."

If pressed, Mama wouldn't flinch in speaking her mind and telling you to stop meddling in affairs that were none of your own. It was her way of shining her light. Dad would tell her that wasn't what Jesus had in mind when he said, "Don't hide your light under a bushel." I always enjoyed Mama's version of the gospel better.

Mama had a fierce determination and one that I shared. When she put her mind to something you could count on it being said or to be done. And that's how I was wired as well. Feeling Mama's grit within, I turned my thoughts back to the plan.

Chapter 19

THANKSGIVING SMACK

"Hackett, I'm glad you came by. And it's always nice to see all the family," Dad said as Joelle and I sat gazing around at the family pictures stirring memories of special moments shared with Mama.

"Good to see you too, Dad." My response seemed so canned, automated, the stuff of mimicry. My mind was not really in the visit which was more recon than heartfelt. I guess I had some of my Dad in me as well. Feeling the whole "life's not fair" sentiment, internally I was just trying to keep my wits about me.

Louie and Kiwi ran off to explore in Dad's office where they enjoyed checking out his Civil War and World War II collectibles. Allie sat on the couch next to Joelle sucking on her thumb and twirling her hair. Dad didn't get Allie. He never really took the time to get to know her. He often would say to me, "I wish Allie would like me. She doesn't have much to do with me." *Smart girl,* even though the thought begged to be spoken, instead I would go easy on him. "Allie has the nature of a cat. She comes around in her own good time."

Now Louie and Kiwi are like golden retrievers that just run up and wag their tails ready to play and explore. Bixie on the other hand is like a temperamental boar that will charge and impale you with its tusks if provoked. And Jett is the cool cat that does his own thing choosing carefully with whom he associates. He and Allie were the most alike in that respect.

"How did Thanksgiving go over at Burt's?" I asked Dad trying to disrupt the awkward silence creeping in the room.

"Oh heck," Dad said quickly becoming agitated. "Spent most of the meal listening to Burt and Sonja go on about how your Mama spoke four different times to Burt. Your Mama hadn't spoken a word the last six weeks of her life, at least not to me. I know doggone well she didn't say nary a word to Burt. They're all a bunch of liars if you ask me. And on top of all the malarkey they were dishing out, they didn't even serve turkey for the Thanksgiving meal. They served ham. I hate ham."

And then I intentionally agitated Dad even more when I added empathetically, "Mama didn't say anything to us either when we visited. She looked as if she was struggling to remain conscious."

"Hackett, your Mama hasn't spoken in six long weeks. Burt is full of it and a dang liar." For some reason Dad felt the need to repeat himself.

"Dad, I wonder if maybe the theology of Burt's church has anything to do with his need to hear voices that aren't there," I said, continuing to stir the Dad's festering pot. Joelle gave me a soft elbow to my side.

"You make a good point Hackett but it doesn't excuse blatant lying."

"Maybe he really believes he heard Mama speaking to him. You know that the core theology of the church he attends revolves around hearing prophetic voices. It's considered spiritual for them to hear voices. They even work themselves up into an emotional frenzy during worship trying to hear something other than themselves yelling out. It's like the greater the emotional frenzy the greater the likelihood that a voice from beyond will speak into their madness. You know the old adage that "if you pray hard enough you might get it" kinda thing. And nothing makes them more inclined to hear voices than talk about the end of times and a prospective soul needing saved on the death bed. An opportunity to flush out a miracle is an opportunity for Burt's halo to shine brighter."

"Well, I don't give a horse-fly what their theology revolves around. It can revolve around Christopher Columbus' keen interest in Biblical prophecies for all I care. I don't believe your Mama said nary a word to anyone over the past six weeks."

I quickly changed the subject as Dad was beginning to go to Defcon 4 and it wouldn't take much to push him to Defcon 5. If Dad was this worked up over the possibility that Mama spoke to Burt before she died and not to him, then God help us all if he found out what I had cooking in the pot.

Chapter 20

GOD'S SALTY BREATH

Burt called and wanted to meet privately at a remote stretch of beach known as "God's Salty Breath". It was a peculiar request which piqued my curiosity. A little paranoia came over me as I began to wonder if somehow Burt was on to me. But I knew that Jett, even if threatened with the pangs of death, would not divulge our clandestine plan to switch Mama's ashes.

So, what was Burt up to? Why did he want to meet? My gut told me he was fishing and I had no intentions of biting. And then other possible reasons began skipping through my mind. Maybe he was wondering about Mama's life insurance and if I knew how much we would all get? Burt and Lucinda both knew Mama favored me so maybe he was trying to discover her monetary worth.

Mama didn't talk about money much. Not even with Dad. She was the only daughter of a very affluent Charlestonian couple. Dad never got along with Pop. It certainly didn't help matters any that Pop never approved of their relationship.

Those two shared bad blood. On more than one occasion Pop called Dad an "oaf". Would absolutely infuriate Dad. Thus the reason why Dad forbade Mama from using a dime of her money to support us in anyway.

The topic of Mama's money was taboo around our house and something we just never talked about. None of us really knew her actual net worth. Mama never brought up the issue of money until more recently when Burt began trying to dip into the family coffers. Love of money was Burt's primary weakness and the chink in his self-righteous armor. And Mama knew it better than anyone.

But to give him the benefit of the doubt, maybe Burt just wanted to catch up on old times without the distraction of family around. I knew this wasn't the case because we always fought growing up. He desired to hang out with me as much as I did with him.

Separated by only ten months with me being the youngest, Dad likened our relationship to that of Esau and Jacob. Maybe Burt was concerned that somehow Mama had schemed to deprive him of his birthright. Who knows? I really didn't care but I was curious as to the sudden interest in meeting.

Arriving at God's Salty Breath, I was shocked at how much the monstrous size dune seemed to have grown in comparison to the last time I had seen it. With panoramic views of the ocean and sound, it was a magnificent, natural sand dune with the thick smell of salt air wafting about inspiring its nickname.

A text message popped up from Burt, "Look up and to your left." I did as instructed and saw a small speck up on top of the sand dune. *Dear God*, I thought. He wanted to meet on TOP of the freaking sand dune. The base rather than the summit on such a cold, crisp day would've been more sensible. Ever the Moses wannabe obviously he desired to meet at the top of the mountain where he imagined God resided.

After climbing up to the top of what seemed like Mount Everest, I dumped a couple loads of sand out of my shoes trying to catch my breath. I stood face to face with Burt. "So, what's up Burt?" I asked beginning to shiver amid the blustery, biting wind that was whipping around us.

"I wanted us to experience together the cleansing breath of God and to clear the air between us."

Why was I not surprised that Burt would try to make a religious experience out of a meeting of the minds. "Well, better salty air than stale church air," I said, trying to make light of the situation. Burt frowned but let the comment slide.

"Seriously, what's up?" I asked again.

"Mama spoke four times when I last saw her."

"What did she say?" I waited with baited breath to hear

how Burt would embellish the infamous last words that were being hotly contested by Dad.

"I love you," Burt said taking great pleasure in vocalizing the words wearing a smirky smile on his face. It was such an annoyingly, self-serving smile that I wanted to ask Burt if he had some Kleenex on him so I could use a few to wipe the cocky, facial expression off his face.

"Good for you Burt. Dad mentioned that you told him that during the Thanksgiving meal. I would advise against bringing it up to him again. It has him just a tad bit annoyed. He's convinced that Mama didn't speak to anyone over the last six weeks. It's probably best to leave that notion unchallenged. At least if you value family peace and well-being."

Burt listened with a blank stare on his face choosing not to respond which was his way of agreeing to disagree. There was an awkward silence. "So, is that what you wanted to tell me?" I asked with a 'you got to be kidding' expression on my face.

"I just thought we needed to share a brother to brother moment to honor Mama's memory. It's what she would have wanted."

No, Mama would want me to ask you to be sure to pay Dad back all the money you've squeezed out of him over the years like juice from an orange. I quickly deleted the thought from my mind.

"I'm glad we could share this moment but couldn't we

have done so maybe in the lobby of the hotel where I'm staying at?"

Burt just returned my gaze with his typical haughty look and then the real reason came out. "What do you know of Mama's small fortune?"

"I think she gave it all to the Greek Orthodox Church in Charleston," I said, trying to get a rise out of Burt. And sure enough, it had the desired effect. Burt's face went blanch white.

"Are you serious?" Burt asked despondently.

"Why wouldn't I be? What else would you expect from such a saintly and generous woman such as Mama? See you at the memorial service Burt," I said turning to leave. I couldn't believe he had the audacity to even broach the subject, especially before final respects had even been observed. But the delicious thought of him remaining behind up on God's Salty Breath assuming the position, in desperate prayer for God to make a way for him to cash in on some of Mama's estate was worth the instigation.

"May God bless you brother," Burt hollered.

"He already has," I replied back over my shoulder already heading down the dune. *He blessed me with Mama.*

Chapter 21

A FAMILY CONSPIRACY

After returning to the hotel I called a meeting of the family tribe in the hotel conference room. It was time to disclose my audacious plan to switch Mama's ashes and to do it before the night of the blood red moon. Well, the upcoming blood red moon didn't have anything to do with it but the more I embellished the plan the more likely the kids would sign on. But we needed to make the switch and to do so soon.

Bixie, Allie, Kiwi, and Louie all came running in from the beach. Louie was soaked, shivering, and teeth a chattering.

"What the heck have ya'll been doing?" I asked.

"Plaa, plaa, play, ay, aying on duh, duh beach," Louie said with chattering teeth. Some things in this world just don't make sense. Like kids who go play in water that is freaking freezing.

"Kids, there is something I want us all to do for ya-ya. It's very important and you will all have a special role. But we only have a small window of opportunity of time. What we are going to do together must take place on the night of the

Blood Moon."

"I, I, I, am so cold," Louie said, teeth chattering overtime. Will it, it, be, be, be, warrrmmm on the Blood Moon?"

"Hackett, the Blood Moon transpired two months ago. The kids are cold and need a hot bath and some warm clothes," Joelle said cutting me off. I took it as a sign that we were to discuss the plan together first. *Works for me*, I thought.

"Bixie, take your brother and sisters up to the room and ya'll get showered and put some dry clothes on. Your Mama and I will be up shortly."

Bixie spared me the tweenie barbs and did what I actually asked of her for a change. Teens rarely do as they're told. That was a sign in and of itself. I just needed to figure out what the universe was trying to tell me. Something was going down and I only hoped that whatever it was, karma was going to deal me a winning hand.

After the kids hurriedly ran off and stepped into the elevator with much laughter and giggling, I looked at Joelle. Before I could say anything she asked, "What's got you acting like a paranoid CIA agent?"

Joelle always had a way of reading me like a book. It was hard to get anything over on her. She picked up on my Bondesque behavior when I was addressing the kids and glancing around the lobby for signs of anyone who might be eavesdropping.

I paused for a moment considering how to most effectively disclose my plan to Joelle. A plan that wasn't fully developed at the moment. I needed her on board. Joelle liked her coffee strong and diluted. So as she gave me her typical "well, out with it" look, I decided to just put it out there.

"Joelle, Dad wants to bury Mama's ashes in the Historic Conundrum County Cemetery. I can't let him to do it. Mama made it clear to me that her remains were to be scattered in Charleston."

Joelle just sat there opposite me wearing her poker face as she is oft to do enjoying when I get all worked up. And as I'm oft to do I just continued. "I'm planning to switch Mama's ashes and I need your help in doing so."

Joelle leaned in and said, "I know. I was wondering when you would bring it up. Anything for your Mama has my full support. I'm all in. Say when and where and I'm there. And the kids will do their part as well."

I beamed from eye to eye and cheek to cheek. In that moment I came to full realization just why Mama loved Joelle so much. Her love was of the kind that inspired the conquering of nations. I was gaining strength of resolve with each wink of her blonde eye lashes. With Joelle on board, I knew that between the two of us a clear plan moving forward would reveal itself. And then I heard the sound of screaming tires and a body-crushing thud coming from the road.

Chapter 22

BUCKMINISTER

Quickly I ran out to the road to see what all the commotion was about. Folks were gathered around something lying on the pavement. Approaching slowly I began noticing blood on the road. An image of a tourist stuck in the grill of a truck flashed through my head but what was actually lying on the road was no tourist. It was a deer. Poor fellow, I thought. He was a huge buck, a twelve pointer. I don't think I had ever seen such a magnificent stag before and certainly not so close to the ocean.

The deer struggled for just a little in obvious pain but then the most mystical thing happened. I'm not sure if Joelle noticed it but I certainly did. It was the closest I had come to experiencing a supernatural phenomenon. The deer possessed a brilliant, azure blue aura that shimmered in the daylight. Lifting its head, the wounded buck looked right into my eyes. There was something strangely familiar about this deer, as if I had seen him somewhere before.

And then as if experiencing a telepathic moment, I heard

the voice of the deer in my head, "I bring a message to you from the netherworld of the Great Spirits. In life, your Mama served our kind with great love and distinction. And so in death, we shall return the favor. I have volunteered to gladly lay down my mortal body to be used as a replacement. My ashes for her ashes. Go now and fulfill your Mama's dying wish to have her ashes scattered among the sacred soil of Charleston. I am Buckminister and now I go to take my place around the sacred fire with your Mama and the other Great Spirits who have gone before."

I was so stunned by the telepathy that I went into free thinking mode, "What is the origin of your name?"

Buckminister let slip his next thought, "Seriously?" And then answered, "It's old English meaning, 'Monastery where deer dwell.'"

Before I could respond, Buckminister stuck his tongue out as if trying to communicate something vocally so I leaned in closer. Joelle grabbed my shirt from behind and pulled me back. "The deer is experiencing the death rattles. This is no time for CPR."

Buckminister's tongue began waggling and shaking violently before his head dropped back to the ground. It was a strange phenomenon to behold but I knew Buckminister was trying to communicate something.

Allie walked up and stood next to me. She tugged on my

shirt and in her soft spoken way said, "Buckminister wants you to also know that the animal spirits have rallied around ya-ya's cause. You will soon receive help from other animal kind to assist with your mission."

Allie doesn't say much. She is quiet as a mouse and more precious than the air you breathe. I wouldn't trade her for all the moonshine in the entire Appalachian mountain range. She spends most of the time with her left thumb in her mouth and the other one twirling her hair. But when she says something it's like when E.F. Hutton speaks, everyone leans in and hangs on every word.

Allie was spot on and indeed had a strong connection with the animal spirits. I looked intently into the mystical looking azure eyes of Buckminister as I watched his spirit energy depart his body. And like a shooting star his blue aura ascended toward the heaven's crossing over to the other side. I was in awe of what I had just experienced and witnessed.

Looking at Allie incredulously I asked, "Did you hear what I just heard inside my head?"

She shook her head in the affirmative as she kept sucking her thumb and twiddling her hair with her other hand. I stood in awe of Allie's psychic powers. Obviously, I had some of my own.

Turning to Joelle I said, "You won't believe what I just witnessed. I heard the deer speak in my head. His name was

Buckminister. I even saw his spirit depart his body. Buckminister's body, eyes, and even its astral energy was as blue as the Pacific ocean."

"Hackett. For Christ's sake. You're wearing your blue tinted Ray-Bans."

I had totally forgotten I had those on. But it didn't matter. It was a powerful moment and I knew clearly what I had to do. I turned back and told everyone to step aside. "I've got this from here on. Don't worry about the deer; he will receive an appropriate memorial service and burial like you would wish for any of your loved ones."

"Watch over Buckminister until I bring the truck over," I said to Joelle. She just raised her right eyebrow with that all-too-familiar expression of, "What the heck do you think you're doing?"

I ran to the truck and drove back over. Dropping the tailgate, I conscripted a gawking tourist standing on the side of the road. He fainted so I had to conscript another one. After I had Buckminister's body in the truck, Joelle and I both got in. Once the doors were shut, I just leaned over the wheel blown away by what had just transpired.

"I know now what we're gonna do," I said to Joelle while staring across the dashboard. "We're going to cremate Buckminister and exchange his ashes for Mama's. And we need to do it before the memorial service. So we've got to act fast."

"So you heard Buckminister's voice in your head?" Joelle asked.

"Did you hear him also?" I replied incredulously. Joelle just smiled and said, "Let's get a move on. The kids will need to be debriefed."

"You never cease to amaze me, my sweet honey smacks," I said, looking into her eyes with an irresistibly flirtatious, lover's gaze. She returned a sexy wink. We were off and running.

Chapter 23

SPIRIT CONNECTIONS

Things could get a little dicey and I knew it. Fortunately, I knew Mr. Stuie Buckley the funeral director but he wouldn't just give me carte blanche access to the cremation chamber, not for the purpose of cremating Buckminister's remains. I'm sure there would be health regulations and an expense involved. I was starting to feel like I was getting in over my head but then Allie gave me a different perspective.

Allie and Mama had a special connection. It's as if they both clearly understood one another. Like a mystical Greek bond that probably could be traced all the way back to King Leonidas 1 of Sparta. The very Greek warrior king who led the famous last stand of the 300 Spartans at the Battle of Thermopylae against the Persian horde. Well some of that kick butt Greek vibe had tracked down through generations of Greeks and landed all up in Allie's gene pool.

Now, as I said before, Allie isn't the boisterous, "hey check me out" type. No, not at all. She abhors attention. She'd rather eat a seven course meal of broccoli and collards than be the center of attention. Allie comes around when she's good and ready and on her own terms. There is no bending Allie to one's will unless something you're offering is appealing and then she may give consideration to the token gift. And that's where some of Allie's Greek comes out. Beware of Greek's who come bearing gifts – yeah, well Allie embodies that saying. She doesn't care if you're of the same tribe or not, she's guarded until you've received clearance.

I never imagined in my wildest dreams that switching Mama's ashes would become far greater than just a son's quest to honor his Mama's wishes. I would quickly learn due in no small part to Allie's psychic connection with animals that Mama's death had captured the imagination of the animal spirits. It was almost like Mama's death had gone viral on some heavenly version of youtube and that now the entire animal kingdom were rallying to her cause, our cause, the cause of the entire created order or so it seemed.

It was too much for my pea-sized brain to wrap around. Tingling sensations began running up and down my arms as goose bumps popped up. I knew that I was experiencing a sort of metaphysical energy that was akin to that of pricking my finger and doing the same to the paw of a cat and comingling blood. I was experiencing the comingling of my spirit with the animal spirits.

Allie had established a connection with the animal spirits

via her psychic powers. I was humbled and yet so proud of her as a father. I now felt a supernatural peace come over me as if all would be well. There were forces at work in this undertaking that knew what they were doing, of that I was fairly certain.

Now as for my role, I was still trying to work all that out. I was always a "show me a sign" kind of person. I needed to see and experience things to tune in and get on the same page. Some folks just think believing comes easy but nothing could be further from the truth. I've suffered as much from doubt as I have from diarrhea. It's almost as if one leads to the other.

And then it happened, a sign. The most majestic bird I'd ever seen landed on the ram thingy on the front of my Dodge truck. And then the first words out of my mouth confirmed what my heart already knew, "Seagle". I didn't know much about how animal spirits operate or how they guide the living but I knew that when messengers were sent that the living would clearly know they had been chosen for a great task. And that I had. Like a spirit guide of sorts, Seagle was sent to guide us on our way.

As I sat there, mesmerized and dumb-founded, in my Dodge cab it became crystal clear, almost magnetically so, that I had been chosen and would also, wield a powerful connection between the living and the dead. Or should I say, between the living and the living because spirits aren't dead. Spirit beings are very much alive less the flesh and bone. Seagle had feathers and seemed very much alive. I'm sure he had blood also. I hate it when my ADD kicks in but I was feeling one with our winged spirit guide.

Chapter 24

SEAGLE

Gathering everyone inside the Dodge Ram, I kind of froze momentarily feeling drawn within. My thoughts began undulating in my mind like a set of waves rhythmically breaking upon the seashore. It was a repetitive crash with the kind of force reminiscent of the ocean's very aquatic power that sends reverberations throughout land and sea. I found myself nearly pulled out of my head by the metaphorical thought as if caught in a cognitive riptide distracting me from the task at hand.

Joelle quickly shook me from my mental meanderings. "Hackett, flap it or strap it."

"Huh, oh yeah. I drifted there for a moment." I got carried away in my thoughts, literally so. I feel so pressed for time that my anxiety is kicking in overdrive as if I'm caught in a mental riptide pulling me away from my task."

"Oh, you're mental alright. Now that you've told us nada about what you were thinking, let's saddle that anxiety and focus it in a productive way," Joelle said. She knew how to keep me focused and on track.

I looked around trying to see if there was any sign of Seagle. I needed direction. "Where are you when I need you? I need a sign to know where to go?" I didn't realize I was speaking out loud.

"Hackett, what are you droning on about? We're heading to the funeral home to do some preliminaries before we break into the cremation chamber," Joelle said losing patience with my less than desirable mental processing rate of speed.

"Yeah, Dad. We have got to go so we can burn up the deer and rescue ya-ya's ashes before the memorial service day after tomorrow," Louie said with a little too much excitement in his voice for my comfort.

"The deer's name is Buckminister," I replied. And then looking over at Joelle I said, "I see you've already debriefed the kids on the mission." It was as if they were already two steps ahead of me the whole time. "How can I keep this clandestine if everybody else knows what we're doing before I even do?"

"Oh Hackett, nobody knows something about anything except for us. We've always been two steps ahead of you. Haven't you figured that out by now? We're family. That's who we are. We sort of know things…about each other."

She just gave me that wry grin of hers and I knew once again why I loved Joelle so much. She is my sugar pie, honey bunch and the cherry on top of my banana split sundae. The sweet in my sweetener and the caffeine in my coffee. She is the shine in my sun and the light in my moon.

And then Allie pointed up toward the sky and there an avian wonder soared in the skies. It was Seagle. "Look!" I cried with a thrill in my voice that startled even Louie who scrambled to look out the window. It was a moment that held our rapt attention as we simply gazed at the graceful strokes of Seagle's wings swooping up and down with such beauty like a very matriarch of the skies.

"Everyone, I'd like to introduce you to our animal spirit guide, Seagle. She's half sea gull and half eagle," I said, trying to educate the little ones about the avian species.

"Hackett, that's an osprey," Joelle said.

"Doesn't matter," I matter-of-factly replied. "The animal spirits have chosen. Seagle leads and we follow. In our desperate hour, when we are weak she will be strong. When we lose our way she will guide us. When we need something she will provide it. We will be sheltered beneath her benevolent wings as we go to fulfill our sacred mission."

"Well, you better start the truck and get moving because Seagle is well on her way to Conundrum County," Joelle said with a hint of sarcasm in her voice.

I felt a tap on my shoulder and Allie just leaned in and whispered quietly in my ear, "Seagle said, 'Go to ya-ya.

Now!'"

I knew that if both Joelle and Allie were speaking truth to my power, then I had to obey the leading of the animal spirits. It was time to embark on an adventure that would prove to be one for the ages. And I for one was ready to earn the Medal of Freedom and dedicate it to Mama's memory.

Chapter 25

RECON

Soaring high above, we followed Seagle's flight path along the winding road leading us deep into the heart of Conundrum County. I had mood music playing enhancing the emotions we were feeling. *Eloi* from *The Time Machine* soundtrack, elicited tingling sensations all over my body. It was a magical, enchanting moment that was almost spiritual. At least I thought so.

Joelle told me to change it. The kids jumped on her SUP board and said, "Yeah Dad, put something else on. And then Kiwi hijacked my iTunes playlist and began playing, *All About That Base* by Meghan Trainor. Everyone including Joelle began experiencing their own kind of spiritual moment. I wasn't feeling it but they were having church.

We drove slightly past the funeral home and turned onto a sandy, dirt road that provided some tree coverage for a recon of the area. It was getting close to the time that the mortician would be knocking off. And then we would rely on stealth to make our way to the funeral home and somehow without being seen, gain entrance and locate the cremation chamber. But first we would need to carry Buckminister's body through the woods and across an open field. It would be dark soon hopefully providing enough concealment for us to cross undetected.

I had faith that if the animal spirits were rallying to Mama's cause then a way would be provided. I would need to be patient and do my part by remaining calm and resolute providing brazen, bold leadership. My clan would be looking to me and drawing inspiration from my courage and determination. Much was counting on how I conducted myself moving forward. I was feeling the pressure but would hold it together at all costs, for Mama and family.

Sure enough there was movement outside the funeral home. It was Mr. Stuie Buckley locking up. *Right on time*, I thought while looking down at my watch. Then I noticed Mr. Buckley do what appeared to be a skip and a dance by his car door yelping something that was unintelligible from my observation point. He reached inside his coat pocket and retrieved something and proceeded to get into his car and hurriedly drove off.

"Interesting," I whispered over to Joelle.

Joelle just raised an eyebrow as she cast a quizzical look my way. "Most of the five businesses in Conundrum County shut down at 5 pm," Joelle said. "Doesn't take James Bond to figure that out."

"It's not James Bond. It's Bond. Hackett Bond," I said, giving Joelle my sexy James Bond impersonation along with a wink.

"Oh Lord." And then she stood up and started walking back to the truck. The goose bumps and tingling sensations must have overwhelmed her. Joelle has always been a softy when it comes to the Bond.

Turning, I hand signaled to Kiwi and Louie who both were leaning against a Pine tree. I pointed two fingers to my eyes and then out toward the funeral home. I'm not sure what they thought I was conveying but Kiwi took off running after Joelle and Louie ran in the opposite direction across the open field adjacent to the funeral home. It was all starting to unravel quickly before my very eyes forcing me to act fast.

Everything went into slow motion as I glanced back at the truck and saw Joelle and Kiwi getting in joining Bixie who never got out to begin with. *Typical*, I thought. No guts, no glory. Where was Allie? I felt like a bobblehead as I just sort of bobbed around until locking my sights on who I was seeking.

Allie was standing off to my right flank, nose to nose with a squirrel who was eye level with her on a tree. Whiskers twitching with two beady eyes deeply entranced with Allie's, they were locked eye to eye in a world of their own. It was as if they were communicating with each other. And then a thought came to me. I needed to get over to Allie to find out if the animal spirits were mounting some type of an assault on the funeral home.

Just as I was rising to my feet Allie turned my way. Her expression spoke volumes. It was a moment that arrested my attention and inspired my imagination. She raised two fingers to her eyes and then pointed directing me toward the funeral home. It was as if the universe had given its consent. It was the sign I had been waiting for.

The funeral home, the very place that typically inspires fear in others only inspired greatness in me. It was time. And I was to lead the charge although Louie had already beat me to the punch making good time crossing the field seeking glory of his own. *That's my boy*, I thought, as a beaming smile broke across my face.

Together, Louie and I would find a way to gain access into the funeral home. Once inside, I would secure the area and then signal for Joelle, Kiwi, and Bixie to bring over Buckminister's body. Something told me that Allie's special powers would be needed once again. My hunch was correct.

Chapter 26

SQUIDITCH

In a mad dash scramble to quickly cross the field I found myself face first on the ground before I even made it twenty yards. It was dark with a recently plowed field that still had its fair share of potholes. I rolled over flat on my back gazing up at a black velvet sky with stars winking down at me. Light from the pale blue moon broke free from a drifting cloud bank casting its illumination all around. It was the break I needed to see my way across but now I could easily be detected by prying eyes. I slowly got up and stealthily continued crossing the field hoping to do so undetected.

Panting considerably from the arduous journey across nearly fifty yards of plowed field, I finally reached the side door of the funeral home. Nearly breathless with my back against the wall, I felt my pulse quickening as the enormity of the situation began settling over me. *This is it*, I thought. I turned to see if Louie was nearby. He wasn't.

The situation now called for me to do what I do best and that was formulating a foolproof, impromptu plan that didn't leave room for error. The enormity of the situation began bursting in my mind like prematurely lit firecrackers in a backseat. The temptation to open the door and jump was real but unfortunately I didn't have the luxury of a vehicle door to jump out of.

Getting Buckminister across the open field and into the funeral home without drawing unwanted attention was the current dilemma I was speedily processing within my tactical brain. An adrenaline rush rifled through me knowing that Joelle was close by and part of the dangerous mission. I wouldn't be honest if I didn't confess that I was stoked to have the opportunity to demonstrate my covert skills which would have her viewing me in a whole new light. I would find a way to get us all inside and she would be both mesmerized and amazed.

Out to impress, I felt top of my game. I just needed to figure out how to get inside without incident. *Where is Louie?* I thought, anxiously looking around for any sign of the bugger. Hearing footsteps I froze momentarily feeling the pounding of the jugular in my neck. It was a quickening that energized me whereas others under similar circumstances would've been rendered immobile by fear.

Rounding the corner of the funeral home was Louie. He was holding something in his hand that rattled like the sound of keys. "What's that in your hand?" I whispered in a raspy voice.

"Keys!"

"Huh?" I asked, somewhat perplexed. And then my heart nearly stopped beating in my chest as I experienced an "oh crap" moment. Headlights were beaming right on me as a vehicle pulled up. "Quick," I said to Louie, having to improvise while cutting our losses. "Run to the woods and don't look back!"

Spinning around in a crouching tiger position, I prepared to face fearlessly my brash opponent. A truck door opened and a shadowy figure jumped out and sort of walked toward me with a sexy sway in the hips. *Wow*! I thought. *These Bond girls are da bomb!* And then the dawn of recognition crystalized. It was Joelle.

Joelle didn't waste any time taking command of the situation. Looking to Bixie who was now at the wheel, she said, "Drive around so we can remove Buckminister from the flatbed. Louie, go unlock the door with the key Allie gave you."

Louie looked at me with a beaming smile across his face. They had the key all along. *But how?* I asked myself. And then I saw a lone figure emerging from the mist that had begun gathering over the field. It was Allie with a squirrel perched on her shoulder twitching its whiskers.

"I gave the keys to Louie," Allie said as if reading my

thoughts. "Squiditch here picked them off Mr. Buckley's person." And then I swear that little critter winked its right eye while twitching its nose up in the air as if he were 007 himself.

"What are you waiting for?" I heard Kiwi say as she peaked around the corner at me. "The door's unlocked. Let's get Buckminister inside."

What magnificent valor! I thought. Heck, what was I worried about. It was one of my proudest moments as a husband and dad. If there was any doubt about the success of the mission it was all but gone now. I gazed at Joelle and said, "Let's go get our sexy on."

"Honey, I already have. Just waiting for you to catch up."

Giving her a love pat on the butt, I hustled to the door feeling once bitten and twice shy. Joelle and the kids were complimenting my skill sets wonderfully. And Squiditch was a keeper. The thought crossed my mind that he probably belonged to a special forces commando team of squirrels, gathering acorns from areas that would cause even the bravest among the squirrel kingdom to cringe in fear.

"Let's do this," I said, shuffling past Kiwi and through the side door.

Chapter 27

HEEBIE JEEBIES

Louie and Bixie flanked the backdoor while remaining in the shadows. Louie owned his role as a spotter scanning the area like a Terminator. Bixie, on the other hand, wore a "whatever" expression across her face, filing her nails wearing earbuds and listening to music while leaning back against the wall. "Don't break a nail at our expense," I whispered unable to restrain the sarcasm. She just rolled her eyes while smacking on gum. Louie would more than compensate for Bixie's mission-challenged state of mind.

The rest of us slid into the funeral home, backs against the wall slithering along scanning for any sign of motion detectors. It was dark and the smell of death permeated the place. Not the rotten corpse kind of smell but the funeral home kind of smell. The smells currently swarming my senses were triggering childhood memories that began assaulting my consciousness. It was enough motivation to be quick about our objective so we could clear the area in short time.

I never liked funeral homes. Growing up, I had to attend

several funerals when Dad laid to rest church folk who had kicked the bucket. Seeing an open casket always gave me the heebie jeebies.

I needed to suck it up and overcome my willies for the sake of the mission. We entered a dark, creepy room like stepping into a black hole not knowing where it would lead. Walking slowly ahead, I walked right into a table that resisted my body. "Flashlight," I said with surgeon like command.

"We don't have a flashlight. You took it out of the truck before we left home," Joelle said with an edge to her voice. "But I have this," Joelle said pulling out her iPhone and igniting the flashlight app.

"Awesome," I replied eagerly taking the cell phone directing the light down at the table shocked to see my handsome, smiling face staring back. It was the chapel altar. For a moment I thought I had passed through some time portal into the future and was seeing the preparations for my own funeral. A weird feeling washed over me as if I was having an out of body experience.

"Slap me," I said turning to Joelle. I didn't have to ask her twice. She hauled off and decked me with a left upper cut to my chin that rattled my teeth and sent me careening to the floor. Hitting with a thud, I began seeing stars with the room spinning like a midnight tornado.

"Daggone it, Joelle!" I said while nurturing my jaw trying

to regain my bearings and stand back up. "A simple slap would've sufficed. I was just wanting to see if I was awake or dreaming."

"Oh, you're awake. But I'd like to try again to see if I am dreaming."

"No," I quickly replied. "You're awake. What is my picture doing on the altar?"

"Hackett, those are pictures of our family on display for your Mama's memorial service."

"Oh," I said. Still it was creepy seeing my face on the altar in the chapel. Then I felt something fury crawling over my right shoulder and I jumped back bumping into Allie who was standing behind me.

"It's just Squiditch," Allie said quietly.

"That squirrel is going to give me a heart attack," I said, trying to regain my composure and relax my heart rate. Squiditch ran across the altar and jumped down crossing the floor to what appeared to be the exit doors leading out of the chapel.

"Follow Squiditch. He knows the way to the cremation chamber," Allie said before putting her thumb back in her mouth.

So we all took off after Squiditch who led us down a darkened hallway which ended at a door with a plaque above it that read, "Got Hope?" *How Dante-esque*, I thought. Kiwi had the phone light and pointed it at the door as I pensively reached over to open it. “Man, this place is weirding me out,” I said, with growing anxiety like a ghostbuster who hadn’t taken his daily dose of meds.

Upon opening the door, stairs greeted us along with a dark abyss. *Great, this keeps getting better*, I thought sarcastically. Making a decision in keeping with courageous, highly effective leaders, I glanced over at Kiwi and Squiditch bravely giving the command, “Lead the way.”

Chapter 28

CHAMBER OF LIFE

Descending into a large room surrounded by cement walls and a dank smell we proceeded with much caution. It was like walking into a ghostly catacomb frequented by Death himself. I certainly hoped he was elsewhere on vacation. I just wanted to take care of business and get out with ashes in hand.

Kiwi found the light switch illuminating the room revealing a cremation chamber with a very large mouth opening wide from inside the cement wall. Then it dawned on me. "We forgot Buckminister," I said, with a stunned expression blanketing my face. Turning to Joelle, she just gave me that "Oh really, you think!?" look along with her typical raised eyebrow.

A creaking sound drew my attention to the chamber door that was beginning to open. What happened next would've made a believer out of an atheist. Squiditch was poised on a small table next to the chamber door with his left paw slightly raised in the air. And then I heard the sound of the upstairs door opening followed by footsteps descending the stairway.

Allie appeared first followed by Buckminister who was walking on all fours. It was a Lazarus-like moment that arrested my attention and left me absolutely mesmerized. "What the…?" I said, as words failed to follow from my open mouth expression.

Allie reached the bottom of the stairs and stepped to the side allowing Buckminister who was walking in venerable fashion with his head held high wearing an angelic-like smile. Instinctively, I did what came natural at the time dropping to one knee, bowing my head in reverence as Buckminister approached. I knew what was taking place. A great spirit was standing before me. I suddenly felt very small.

"Rise my friend," Buckminister said as his ethereal spirit illuminated the room in a brilliant white light. "I have lived long upon the earth. The twelve points on my antler attest to the truth I speak. But my time has come and so I gladly take my place with your Mama and the other Great Spirits. The physical body before you is but ashes and dust. Use it as you will. Your Mama saved my hide more than once so I gladly offer mine up to fulfill her wishes. Do not look upon this room as a chamber of death but rather a chamber of life. For now I depart in death but go beyond to live again." And with those words Buckminister's spirit vanished.

Standing before me was Jett with a huge buck sprawled across his shoulders and Elvis who leapt up with his forepaws on my chest giving me a big old wet one. "I could use some help," Jett said straining under the weight.

Momentarily stunned and confused, I wasted no time lending a hand. "Sure," I said, rising to my feet suddenly remembering that a corpse is usually placed inside a box or coffin for the cremation. "Hold on," I said while quickly looking around until I found what I was searching for. Spotting a large cardboard box, I grabbed it while quickly manipulating it the best I could. Jett and I then placed Buckminister's body inside it with his magnificent twelve point antler protruding out. Before shutting the chamber door I called for a moment of silent thankfulness for Buckminister's sacrifice on Mama's behalf.

Closing the door I looked over and saw Squiditch perched by the controls. I gave Allie the nod. She glanced over at Squiditch who hit the power switch igniting the furnace. The red light eventually turned green at which time I opened the door and slid the drawer out. Heat wafted through the room followed by the most aromatic scent of Plumeria's and Lehua blossoms from Hawai'i. It was a heavenly scent.

"It is finished," I said, with a reverent tone to my voice. "Grab the plastic bag over there on the table," I said to Kiwi. "Let's get the ashes in the bag and don't drop even a dust particle. Treat Buckminister's ashes as you would ya-ya's own."

It was a spiritual experience we all shared and one that I would never forget. I don't know what everyone else saw but as for me I know what I saw. A miracle unfolded before my very eyes in that chamber. A selfless deer known as Buckminister brought new meaning to "ashes to ashes, dust to dust" with a death walk that inspired faith and kindled hope in the soul, a hope for which I would be forever grateful to the animal spirits.

Chapter 29

ANIMORA

Back at the hotel, I spent a restless night listening to whispering winds and an occasional glimpse of what appeared to be a moving shadow. Eventually I drifted off entering another dimension of consciousness more like a vision than a dream. It was like an out of body experience where I saw myself asleep on the bed and then hurtling along at the speed of light through a long, dark tunnel rapidly approaching a flaming fire at the other end. Couldn't help but think I had died and was heading for the fires of Hell. But upon reaching the other end, I was pleasantly surprised.

I quickly found my feet and began walking amidst a mystical jungle that was as mesmerizing as it was serene. The trees were gargantuan like something out of the prehistoric age. Thick, lush foliage wrapped around the base of the trees and the most luminous, multi-colored lights pervaded the jungle's interior. Lost in wonder, any residual fears I had felt quickly dissipated. A great camp fire began crystallizing in my sights as I drew nearer.

A rustling of foliage and the sound of footsteps from the other side of the camp site arrested my attention. Stepping out into the midst of a small clearing, I shuffled uneasily trying to follow the sound that seemed to echo all around. And then an uncanny stillness came over the jungle as if all living things were acting in concert ceasing and desisting from all sounds.

Peering out from the panoramic vista of trees and shrubbery were animals of every breed imaginable even those long extinct. I was standing in the midst of Heaven and had the very real sensation that I had been summoned by the Great Spirits of which the vast majority were animals. Mama was right, I thought in amazement.

And then I heard the rustle of foliage and for some reason I expected a lion to emerge and walk out into the clearing. But it was a raccoon with the most brilliant blue eyes I had ever seen. He walked with such poise and carried himself in a sage-like manner. Realizing I was in the presence of greatness, I instinctively dropped to my knees touching the ground with my nose. I did not dare look up until summoned to do so.

"Rise," I heard a voice say. I didn't know if the voice was in my head or if the raccoon had actually spoken. But immediately I felt myself rising to my feet as if being assisted by an otherworldly force of some kind. My eyes looked upon the raccoon getting an eye full of his shimmering fur that rippled in the astral light. He wore a bone white robe and was leaning on a rowan staff. Surely at one time he was Yoda's Jedi master, I thought incredulously. The mannerisms were so uncanny.

"Who are you and where am I?" I asked trying to reconcile my disbelief with what my eyes were seeing and my ears were hearing.

"I am Rally. You have been summoned to the Spirit Fire of Animora by the Great Spirits."

"Is this animal Heaven?"

"There is no animal Heaven." The great raccoon spirit replied. "There is just Heaven. And you stand where few other mortals have stood. Welcome to Animora, the kingdom of creatures great and small."

"I have many questions to ask and don't know where to begin."

"Filled with questions are we? Answers you seek. And answers you will discover in time. But for now you must sit at the Spirit Fire and breathe the sacred smoke."

Rally approached the circular stone pit, inviting me to join him by the sacred flames which blazed and flickered in hues of purple and blue. Taking my place opposite Rally, I was keenly aware that the flames didn't emit any heat although the fire blazed with intensity.

Rally just sort of sat there in silence while gazing into the fire. Something told me not to speak unless spoken to. After what seemed an eternity, Rally finally broke the silence.

"Your Mama once sat where you're sitting now. She was but a child at the time of only seven mortal years. One of my kind was but a young one sojourning among the mortal kind. It was his first encounter with the worst and the best of the human kind. Caught in the crosshairs of a hunter, your Mama stepped in front of his sites and never flinched. Her compassion and love did not go unnoticed. As a result of her actions, the voice of the Great Spirit echoed across Animora, 'A mortal after my own heart.' She lived her mortal life with honor and conducted herself with dignity. Her remains are to be taken to the crescent harbor and scattered among the sacred elements."

Rally then peered through the flames with eyes of sapphire that arrested my attention. I sat fixed to the ground locked in Rally's gaze knowing I was sitting in the presence of sheer intelligence and cunning. I dared not speak, but listened intently as his next words seemed to bore into my soul.

"Fulfill your purpose and set your Mama's spirit free. All will be revealed in time." And then flames shot out from his eyes and drew me into the Spirit Fire as the sacred flames swirled all around me. Closing my eyes and cringing in fear of the flames, I found myself lying back in my hotel bed with only the sound of crashing waves greeting my ears.

Startled, I looked around beholding only the light of a pale moon shimmering across the surface of the waters. Joelle was snoring and still very much in sleep land. I just sat up in awe and wonder as I recalled the vision. It was so real and vivid that I knew I had actually crossed over.

In stunned amazement, I felt reinvigorated to finish what we had started. I knew exactly where this crescent harbor was located. It was the place Mama loved to frequent the most back on Sullivan's Island; one of Charleston's island towns.

As I got out of the bed and walked out onto the balcony I gazed out at a crescent moon that twinkled in the starry night sky. Peace enveloped me as Rally's words crashed over my consciousness like the ocean waves were upon the surf, "All will be revealed in time."

Chapter 30

FLIPPIN' AND A FLOPPIN'

We arrived early at the funeral home and were met by Mr. Buckley at the door. He was a genteel fellow with a Santa physique. We exchanged a few pleasantries and then he led us into the chapel. The smell of fresh fragrant flowers filled the room drawing our attention to the front where the altar was positioned with pictures flanking a plain wooden urn with Mama's ashes inside. True to form and ever the cheapskate, Dad had selected the most inexpensive wooden urn available to house Mama's ashes. *Geez*, I thought. *How predictable.*

There was also an assortment of violet blue dyed flowers made in the shape of a purse. *Interesting*, I thought. Reminded me of my younger years when Mama would grab her favorite blue suede purse and head off with her lady friends. I had forgotten all about those times but just figured it was her special occasion purse and never thought anymore of it. But I was soon to learn something about my Mama that I had never known. And the blue suede secret would soon be let out of the bag. No pun intended.

I quickly glanced back at Allie who was lingering by the door with her thumb in her mouth. But no sign of the plastic bag with Buckminister's ashes. I was starting to stress.

"And over here is where we've placed your mother's urn," I heard a voice say. *Really? You think?* I thought to myself. It was Mr. Buckley giving us the chapel tour while I was mentally preoccupied with the mission at hand. I glanced over at Joelle who was giving Mr. Buckley her ear while I was feigning politeness as my palms were starting to sweat. We'd come so far and I didn't want to screw it up at this point.

Where were Buckminister's ashes? I thought, really starting to get irritated. *And where is that shifty squirrel when I need him?*

Kiwi came into the chapel through the side door and was carrying the plastic bag of ashes. I immediately distracted Mr. Buckley and drew his attention away from the front of the chapel. "I really want to thank you for the letter of support you wrote to Bishop Miniger back when I faced off with him over trying to move my Dad to a new church appointment. It was nice to know that someone had my back as well as the Bishop's ear so my words weren't held against my Dad."

"I was glad to do it," Mr. Buckley said with a big beaming smile on his face.

I glanced back over my shoulder and saw Joelle, Kiwi, Louie, and Allie all gathered by the altar with their backs to us. Joelle slipped a plastic bag into her tote bag. It was done. I was overcome with emotion. Mr. Buckley was saying something about his bible study group that he had been leading with nearly twenty-five folks in attendance and I just started tearing up.

"But you don't have to attend," he said feeling horrible that he had upset me. "I was just trying to share about the success I am having in getting folks to attend bible study."

"It's not the bible study," I replied wiping tears from my eyes. "It's Mama."

"I'm so sorry for your loss," Mr. Buckley said almost seeming relieved while trying to be comforting when suddenly Squiditch jumped up onto his shoulder. "Dear God," Mr. Buckley hollered as he jumped back flipping over a pew bench.

Squiditch was up to something but I couldn't exactly tell what. Maybe it was just Mama having her way with the moment. I was starting to believe it could just about be anything. And then I heard a booming voice, "What's going on in hear?" Turning I saw Dad standing in the doorway with a furrowed brow wearing a look of damnation itself across his face.

"It seems we have a squirrel on the loose in the chapel," Mr. Buckley said as I helped him to his feet.

"A what?!"

Repeating himself somewhat embarrassed, Mr. Buckley

said, "A squirrel."

"There is a squirrel running around in here?" Dad said astonishingly as anxiety flooded his countenance. Not one to take kindly to unexpected surprises, Dad was instantly flustered. "Well, we need to get that pesky squirrel out of here before folks begin gathering. It's a desecration to the sacred space."

"It's ok Dad," I said, trying to calm him down.

"The heck it is!" Dad fired back.

Squiditch then leapt up on the altar and sat perched atop Mama's wooden urn. He swished his tail a time or two, flailed his arms out and swayed side to side before leaping down and scurrying out the side door.

"You have to admit Dad. Mama would be getting a kick out of that squirrel," I said.

"She sure would," a voice said entering the chapel. It was Lucinda with her husband Phinn in tow. And from my vantage point things were about to get real interesting.

Chapter 31

FAMILY DRAMA

Lucinda was dressed to the nines, sporting make up, and wearing God-awful, black sunglasses. Never had I seen her with so much makeup caked all over her face. *Good Lord*, I thought. For such a plain Jane, I was a little thrown by the dramatic makeover.

Reminded me of a story I heard about a woman who supposedly asked Billy Graham, "Is it a sin to put on makeup?" To which he replied, "If the barn needs painting, paint it."

Well, Lucinda had nearly rehabbed her face and I wasn't so sure it was for the better. Rarely the one to wear makeup, Lucinda was your typical homely recluse who seldom ventured out of her burrow. But this was a Lucinda on a mission and my wheels were quickly turning trying to figure out just who it was she was trying to impress.

"I see you have my high school picture on display?" Lucinda said to Dad as she strutted upfront like a peacock in her colorful dress in hues of purple, blue, and green. Mama's favorite colors. I hadn't even noticed but there it was as if she were the one who died. Resting on an easel was her high school pic residing in a 24 x 36 gold trimmed frame.

"You've got to be kidding," I said, letting slip my thought while glancing around to see if there was any sign of her former boyfriend in the chapel.

Turning my way with a cutting look on her face Lucinda retorted, "What was that Hackett?"

I just waved my hand in the air and replied, "I was just commenting about the blood-sucking mosquito that whizzed by my ear."

Lucinda simply turned back to her picture as if enamored with it. There wasn't any doubt in my mind that she had asked Dad to prominently display her high school picture with the other family pics in hopes that her long, lost love who had dropped her like a hot potato would show up to Mama's memorial service. Her former lover, Billy Swan had gone on to become one of Conundrum County's prominent business leaders. And Lucinda wasn't missing an opportunity to rekindle a flame in an ember that had long since grown cold.

Poor Phinn, I thought. He'll never measure up to Billy. And I'm sure Lucinda's filled his ears over the years with how princely, perfect Billy was.

Slipping out the door, I went looking for Joelle as more

family and friends began gathering. Walking down the hall I spotted Louie bending over with his butt up in the air as guests began to enter. "Louie," I chided. "Butt down and head up." Having too much fun Louie just sprung back up and cackled as he ran down the hallway.

What is up with Louie and his preoccupation with butts and poop? I thought. *Must be post pull-ups partum he's experiencing or something to that effect.*

"Hey, where is your Mama?" I hollered after him.

"Taking a poop," he hollered back over his shoulder not missing a beat as he scampered off to a side door leading outside.

Allie strode up beside me. "Mama is waiting on you outside by the truck with Jett."

"Ok, hang out with your Grandpa until I get back." But before I could leave a booming, bombastic voice belted out, "Hackett, how the heck are you, you son of a gun?"

Every head in the chapel nearly experienced whiplash from turning so quickly toward the sound of the irreverent voice. It was Uncle Titus, Mama's brother. Things were about to get lively.

Chapter 32

TITUS AND KING JAMES

Titus swept me up in a burly bear hug nearly squeezing the life out of my body. Felt like I was about to depart and join Mama along with the other Great Spirits. After turning several shades of blue I collected myself as Titus set me down. Then he slapped me on the back knocking me into ninety-year old Serelda, a former parishioner of Dad's. She went sprawling to the floor with a yelp.

It had been nearly ten years since I'd seen Titus. He always thought I was the rich one in the family. God knows where he got that idea. I made my living in the dot com business designing and selling paternity wear for men with 'man boobs' and 'barrel bellies'. I also dabbled in writing with one bestseller to boot. But Joelle is probably the reason they think I'm loaded. It's the mystery that keeps on giving.

"So how has that sexy woman of yours been treating you lately?" Titus asked with a wry grin breaking across his rowdy face. His smile revealed a missing canine tooth. *Better than you, let me tell you,* I thought.

Lacking couth and class, Titus was night and day from Mama. Boisterous, rude, and direct; a drinker not a thinker. He was the kind of person that gave voice to his crass thoughts and often without restraint or care. Before I could respond, Burt's sixteen year old son Samuel walked up and tapped me on the shoulder. *Oh Boy*, I thought. *Stuff just keeps getting better.*

Burt and Sonja along with the rest of their clan in tow: Ruth, Rebekah, Gideon, and Jude, all circled around. Burt really took the Bible stuff seriously and his kids names were a testament to that fact.

"God is smiling down on Mama," Burt said joining the blissful conversation. "Bless you brother," Burt said reaching his hand out to Titus. Wanting to gag, I felt like I was in a monastery with a monk wannabe.

"Well, I'll be an angel's uncle, if it isn't Saint Burt himself who has condescended to grace us with his presence," Titus belted. I noticed that Burt anticipated Titus' aggressive welcoming style as he immediately raised and opened up his big black King James bible, stopping Titus in his tracks before he could get his arms wrapped around him. You would've thought Titus was a vampire and Burt was wielding a crucifix by the way Titus back stepped and quickly excused himself as he went off to mingle with other family and friends that were gathering.

"Smooth as molasses," I said to Burt.

"Works like a charm. Titus never cared for the Word more than he does for the absurd. But he can't keep dodging it but for so long."

"I hear you," I replied not quite sure if Burt was in one of his salvific moods with Titus in his soul-saving crosshairs. I couldn't help but ask, "How much longer do you think he'll keep dodging?"

"God and the angels above know that his time is running out. Today is the day of salvation and how fitting for him to receive the Word of salvation here at Mama's memorial service. Yes, dear God bless us all, the gathered will hear a great word on this day."

I suddenly felt the urge to pass gas, more from anxiety than from a biological need. The gathering was turning into a perfect storm of family drama that was unraveling by the minute. I was just hoping I could hold everything together long enough to give Mama a grand send off – to Charleston soil that is.

Walking over to Joelle who was talking to an older lady holding a blue suede purse, I leaned in close and whispered, "I need to tell you something."

A little annoyed by the interruption, she replied, "What is it, Hackett?"

"I see dumb people."

Joelle gave me that stern look that I must've seen a thousand times, the kind that sort of pulls you up quick and inspires you to mosey on along.

Chapter 33

ELVIS AND THE SQUAWKERS

The chapel was brimming with people sitting on pews and congregating in the aisle. I looked around to see if I could put my eyes on Dad to make sure he was calming down from his encounter with Squiditch. He was standing by the side entrance to the chapel talking to Mr. Buckley; probably about the consternation Squiditch had caused him.

"Oh my," I heard someone say. *What now?* I thought while turning back to the front entrance of the chapel. I was starting to feel like Chief Brody in the movie Jaws. For a gathering such as this, there was commotion of an unusual sort with a rippling through the throng of people who were quickly clearing aside from the center of the aisle.

"Dear God, it's a beaver!" Matilda Simpson a middle age widow shrieked throwing herself in desperation into the arms of Randolph Emerson an older gentleman who was very much single. He returned his newfound lover's enthusiastic overture by wrapping his arms around her and planting a big, wet one on her lips. She hauled off and slapped him much to his bewilderment.

"It's a bear!" Theresa Stiles screamed as she fainted into the arms of Jethro Hillings who was beside himself with excitement as he tried to lay eyes on the bear while dropping Theresa to the floor. "Let me through," Jethro belted pushing through the panic stricken squawkers. "I need to go get my gun out of the truck."

"Gun?" Someone hollered in response.

"Someone's got a gun," was now the word quickly spreading to the front of the chapel. Folks who were seated began to jump up as pandemonium erupted. Scanning the aisle, my eyes locked on the moving target which was a sight for sore eyes. "Come here, oh boy," I said, as Mama's dog, Elvis ran and leapt up into my arms giving me lots of slobber on the collar.

"It's just Elvis," I said, attempting to restore calm to the situation.

"Elvis is alive and in the chapel!" I heard a lady yell to folks rushing out of the chapel knocking Dad over a potted plant and sprawling down onto the floor. *So much for order and calm*, I thought, watching Dad turn several shades of red while quickly getting back up on his feet. Folks were now turning to rush back into the chapel desperately wanting to get a glimpse of Elvis Presley.

"He's RISEN," someone shouted!

But what people heard upfront was, "He's Pissin'!" Folks began jumping up trying to avoid Elvis for fear that he was going to whiz on their Sunday best. It was mayhem as people started rushing up the aisle causing much confusion and a collision of bodies.

Dad was now absolutely beside himself. "What the heck is Elvis doing running loose in the funeral home?" I couldn't help but take a devilish delight in Dad's ire. It was almost as if Mama and the animal spirits were pushing Dad's buttons. A smile slipped from my lips which didn't go unnoticed.

"You finding something humorous?" Dad snipped swiveling his head about trying to put eyes on Elvis. His mood became darker by the moment.

"Dad, I told Jett to bring Elvis to the memorial service. You know Mama would have it no other way. And she would want Elvis sitting on the front pew with the rest of us. Matter-of-fact, truth be told, Mama would value the last respects of the animal kind more so than that of some of the folks showing up."

Before Dad could fire off a response, we both spotted Squiditch up on the chapel podium looking down over the urn. Mr. Buckley entered from the side door hobbling along as quickly as he could move his bulky frame. "Shoo, shoo!"

Squiditch hopped down on top of the urn and gave his tail a quick swish and then ran straight for us. I stepped to the side and Dad just froze in place and said, "Dear God!" Rally ran right between his legs and parted a pathway through the screaming attendees who were by this point beside themselves in alarm and dismay. Like Moses parting the Red Sea, Squiditch enjoyed a straight path to the front door scurrying outside. Elvis just sort of cocked his head while raising his left leather watching Squiditch make a run for it.

I glanced over at Dad and lost it, belting out with laughter. He just glared at me and said, "There's no reverence in you." And then he quickly joined Mr. Buckley who was hobbling up the aisle to calm the frightened guests.

Where is a bottle of Devil's Cut when I need it? My thought was interrupted by the bald headed Bishop who came strolling into the chapel. It was Bishop Jack Daniels who everyone called Bishop JD. Although of no relation to the whiskey maker, Bishop JD certainly lived up to his name. I headed over to extend my warmest hypocritical regards and appreciation for the Bishop accepting my Dad's invitation to conduct Mama's memorial service.

We exchanged a few pleasantries and then I got to the point. "What has Dad instructed regarding the service?"

"He's requested that I observe communion and open the floor afterwards for a few testimonials. Burt will begin the time of remembrance." *Perfect*, I thought. "What about the scripture reading?"

"He didn't request any particular scripture. I've picked something out from Ecclesiastes."

Sounded like Dad was being true to form as if he were planning his own funeral. Nothing thus far had Mama's staple marks on it.

"Well, you might want to read Psalm 139 as it was Mama's favorite."

"Do you have everything squared away for communion?" I asked.

"Yes, I have asked the pastor Rev. Jose Mario to prepare the sacraments."

And then a delicious thought entered my scheming mind. Bishop JD had a reputation for the drink. The perfect alibi for what I had in store. I pulled out my smart phone and tweeted a text over to Jett, smiling with devious intent. "Need a bottle of JB asap."

Chapter 34

COMMUNION SHOTS

After restoring order in the chapel both Bishop JD and Rev. Mario led the family down the aisle during the processional signifying the start of the memorial service. Elvis strolled in wagging his tail behind Jett casting a "whoomp, there it is," cocky look over at Jethro who returned a stern glare holding his shotgun tightly to his side feeling gypped out of an opportunity to get him a bear.

Rev. Mario read a scripture from the Book of Revelation with a thick Hispanic accent. Mama had told me about the new preacher at their church who was difficult to understand and how she would just nod, "Yes", when he spoke to her. His primary language was Spanish with English clearly a distant second.

The church Mama and Dad had attended after he retired a few years earlier was a simple, rural church with only a hand full of folks attending keeping the Historic Conundrum Church doors open. Mama came up with every excuse imaginable to miss the Sunday services. She would often joke with Dad, "You go right ahead to the Conundrum Church but Jesus and I are going to the beach to worship and listen to a choir of gulls sing the Gloria Patri."

After reading over the last minute change written on a note handed to him from the Bishop, I overheard Rev. Mario leaning over and asking him if reading the entirety of Psalm 139 was correct. Of course, I had purposefully left out the fact that Mama's favorite verses of Psalm 139 didn't include verses 19-22. Oops. Chuckling at the thought, I received a stiff elbow to my side from Joelle.

As Rev. Mario read through the Psalm he put special emphasis on Psalm 139: 19-22 NIV, "If only you, God, would slay the wicked! Away from me, you who are bloodthirsty! They speak of you with evil intent; your adversaries misuse your name. Do I not hate those who hate you, Lord, and abhor those who are in rebellion against you? I have nothing but hatred for them; I count them my enemies."

Several "amens" were heard in the chapel, mostly from Burt's clan. Turning several shades of red and shuffling uneasily in the pew, Dad kept his eyes fixed on the floor growing more agitated by the moment. Things were clearly not going anywhere close to what he had planned or envisioned for Mama's memorial service. As Rev. Mario finished the reading you could hear a pin drop. I glanced over and noticed that Burt was nodding his head in the affirmative as Rev. Mario plowed through the odious words as if he had written the verses himself. Religion and wrath are like mash potatoes and gravy, they taste good to those who have a hankering for some judgmental drama.

The cell phone vibrated in my suit pocket. I pulled it out and read a text message from Jett. It was short and sweet. "Devil's Cut in play." I smiled and looked up after sending my response. "That's my boy."

Rev. Mario rambled through the communion liturgy. I told him to keep it short and only give us the concentrated version. Dad was becoming more annoyed by the minute. We all headed up front in a single file line as we received a wafer and a small, shot-sized communion cup that folks assumed contained grape juice. Jett had put a drab of color dye in the chalice filled with Jim Beam's Devil's Cut. Like liquid fire from the gods it went down smooth but lit up the senses, spiritual and all. If expressions could speak there would've been some hootin' and a hollarin' going on around that chapel.

Rev. Mario winced after throwing back the communion cup anticipating the sweet taste of Welch's Grape Juice. He wore an expression across his face as if he were being baptized in lemon juice. Bishop JD, on the other hand, kept his poise almost naturally so as if the bourbon whiskey from the communion cup was purging his physical temple of all traces of wickedness within.

Some of Mama's friends were enjoying themselves as Dalia, one of her closest slipped back in line toward the back for another round. Dad, who was seated to my left leaned over and said, "Someone got into the communion juice. I've never tasted such. What the heck is going on?"

"Could've been a bad batch of grapes," I whispered reassuringly. "I've tasted worse."

Dad just grunted as he nervously twitched his glasses with his left hand. We were ready now for the testimonials as Rev. Mario hurriedly wrapped up the communion service. Upon opening the floor, Burt stood and walked to the front. I leaned over to Joelle and said, "This should be good."

Chapter 35

MILLIE AND MAMA

Peppering the chapel like swaying reeds in the wind were a bunch of light weights possessing a low tolerance for alcohol. There were a lot of smiling faces with pleasant memories of Mama enhanced by the communion shots. But then there was Millie whose taste for the drink was fanned into flame by the shot of bourbon whiskey during communion. As Burt stood and made his way to the front I noticed Millie sitting across the aisle one pew back from the left front stealing a quick sip from her whiskey flask.

Gracefully refined and dressed like a southern belle, Millie was seventy-two going on fifty-two. She was the life of a party. Bringing a smile to my face was the incident that evoked another "Dear God Annabelle" moment from Dad. Millie was the personification of great consternation for Dad.

A few years back Millie and Mama went on a road trip to Memphis to visit Graceland. While there they got into a heap of trouble by jumping on a couple of horses at Elvis' Graceland Stable. They rode like lightning out of a bottle hurdling Elvis' white fence blazing a trail across the neighborhood streets until they were finally subdued by the local police. Making the local 6 pm news in Memphis, Millie and Mama were all smiles as they were cuffed and put into the cop car. Of course, Millie had a flask on her person and the cops were in bit of quandary as whether to charge her with a DUI or not.

To say the least, Dad was irate when he received a call from Memphis' finest regarding Millie and Mama's shenanigans. Mama stood by her story that the horse had a mind of its own and was dead set on leaping out of the corral and running free. Millie backed her play and took great delight in the equestrian drama. To make matters worse, Millie and Mama got hold of their mugshots and had them made into postcards mailing more than a few out to family and friends.

The Memphis escapade always came up during holiday gatherings but we had to keep our comical thoughts on the matter under wraps when Dad would enter the room. Mama and Millie's antics in Memphis riled Dad in a bad way as he was very meticulous about preserving the family image ever trying to maintain an air of having the model family for good church folk to aspire. Well, Mama saw fit to shatter that image with us kids following suit. She always said, "Having fun is about living life the way it was meant to be lived."

That's why Mama gravitated to friends like Millie. Together they were like chicken and barbeque sauce.

I certainly was hoping Millie would get enough drink in her to stand up and share a memory of her and Mama. I knew Dad was thinking the exact opposite. My dream moment would be his nightmare. Mama's friends were Dad's foes. Funny how life works out that way sometimes for a couple. At least it did for Mama and Dad. He always tried to be prim and proper for the church's sake while Mama belonged to outlaw heaven ever shooting from the hip.

All eyes were on Burt as he took his place behind the pulpit. And then the transformation took place as he morphed from Mama's son to Mama's savior. I knew what was coming as an insatiable thirst for some Devil's Cut made my knees start bouncing. Joelle slammed her left hand down on my knee sending a clear message for me to give Burt my undivided attention. She could certainly be touchy feely when she wanted. That was for sure. And not the kind of touchy feely that sparked a fire of desire.

Chapter 36

BURT'S SOUL TALK

I don't know if you've ever heard someone pass gas in a church service but when it happens your thoughts are not exactly on the Virgin Mary. It was the worst smelling fart ever. I couldn't discern whether it emanated from Bishop JD, Rev. Mario, or Burt but it was a doozy. We were definitely downwind because the smell hit my nose like a hard, slanting rain from the front. I was willing to wager it was Burt because as a kid he'd pass gas when he became anxious or excited.

Burt had been chomping at the bit to testify at Mama's memorial service. I had a good idea what Burt was going to say and my gut was right. True to form, Burt started with an emphatic "Mama's in a better place now." His clan and a few others belted out in the affirmative, "Amen!"

Great, I thought. *Here we go.* I didn't know what was worse, the smell of a silent but deadly one or Burt's soul talk. He lost me at "Mama's in a better place now." It summed up Burt's theological substance, shallow as a tide pool on a beach during low tide. And it summed up his relationship with

Mama. Basically absentee throughout much of his adult years. Oh, but he would give the royal treatment to Sonja's parents while having little to do with Mama and Dad unless he needed more money. Then they could bank on him coming around to pay a visit. But Mama was nobody's fool. She saw through Burt's monkeyshines.

Burt's testimony was supposed to be about memories of Mama. But of all his lifetime memories of Mama, Burt chose his last. He droned on about his last visit with Mama.

"I needed to make sure that Mama was right with the Lord," Burt said while getting all teary eyed.

I wanted to put a finger in my mouth and gag. Restraining from shaking my head since I was sitting up front, I rolled my eyes instead. Bishop JD was looking right at me as if sitting in judgment. From the look on his face, I felt he was preoccupied with suspecting me of switching out the communion juice. I had always been viewed by the powers to be within the denominational church of being a renegade, rebel, and rogue. In a show of defiance, I passed some gas of my own.

Burt was just getting started as he continued, "After praying the sinner's prayer for Mama, I asked if she were in agreement and she nodded yes. She then said six times, 'I love you.'"

Wait a minute, I thought to myself. He told Dad at the

Thanksgiving meal that Mama spoke four times. My thoughts began to focus on Burt's inconsistencies. I could feel the heat rising in Dad's cheeks with each word that Burt uttered.

"I needed to know for myself," Burt repeated for emphasis, "that Mama and Jesus were one in heart, mind, body, and soul. I needed to know for me," he said tempering his words with a touch of self-deprecation.

Well, I thought sardonically. *God certainly didn't bless you with long term memory recall.* I kept waiting to hear Burt share a REAL memory of Mama that predated his last one but nada. He finished by imploring everyone in the room to, "Search your hearts and make sure you find Jesus there. Praise God! Amen."

Burt stepped down and I noticed that Dad was twitching his head with the same tick he always had when anxious or angry. I knew there would be words between Dad and Burt after the graveside to follow. Before I could rise to share my testimony Jett beat me to the bunch. He had the fire of his Dad in his belly. I could only imagine what he was about to say in response to Burt's testimony about the state of Mama's soul. As if any of us, besides Burt, ever had a lingering doubt.

Chapter 37

JETT AND MAMA

Jett commanded the floor proffering a personable and down-to-earth remembrance of Mama which was a welcome respite from Burt's religious rhetoric and pretentious airs. Jett's words seemed to have a relaxing effect on Dad as his once clenched fists were now opening like Morning Glory flowers.

"Ya-ya was all about the animals. One of my earliest recollections about her was when she gave me a subscription to *National Geographic Kids* that included a deck of animal cards. It always stuck with me her love of animals. It shaped how I came to view animals and I've been an animal lover ever sense. I got that from ya-ya."

Elvis gave a short howl in the affirmative. Snickers were heard around the chapel. Dad just cast a stern look down the pew but Elvis just gave him a flap of his ear while keeping focus on Jett hanging on his every word.

A blue jay alighted outside on the window sill as Jett continued speaking. Twitching its head about the blue jay seemed drawn to Jett's testimony. There was something mysteriously wonderful about the blue jay's presence as if Mama were somehow present. It was apropos since Mama was like a contemporary Saint Francis of Assisi when it came to the animals.

"Ya-ya worked for many years as an assistant at the local animal shelter. I remember on one occasion going with my Dad to visit the shelter. Ya-ya took me to a room where she had been nursing back to health a little blue jay who had suffered a broken wing. She asked me to walk with her outside to the back of the shelter where she carried the blue jay ever so gently in her hands. She lifted the blue jay up to her face, eye to eye as she spoke the following words that I've never forgotten. She said, 'Take these broken wings and learn to fly again, learn to live so free, hear the voices sing and the book of love will open up and let you in.'" And then ya-ya smiled as she handed the blue jay to me said, "You release him."

"When I released that blue jay something in me soared along with it. I was mesmerized by the experience of having been part of helping a creature once broken being made whole again. That experience was made possible because of ya-ya who was larger than life with a big heart filled with love for the animals. Of course, I learned later that the words she spoke was from one of her favorite songs Broken Wings by

Mr. Mister." A few chuckles reverberated around the chapel.

"Didn't matter," Jett continued with a sweeping grin across his face and a tear trickling down his cheek. "She made the lyrics her own and I'm sure it became an anthem of life for that little blue jay. That is how I shall always remember ya-ya. One who loved animals as passionately as she loved life. Love you ya-ya."

Jett walked back over to take a seat and I stood before he could do so and gave him a hug. Looking up over Jett's shoulder I saw the blue jay still perched on the window sill and couldn't help but wonder if the blue jay was a descendant of the one Mama helped heal.

Glancing back over at Allie, I noticed she was all smiles returning my gaze. I knew she had made some kind of connection with the blue jay. When I turned back the blue jay had flitted off. A peaceful, easy feeling came over me as I felt Mama's presence. It was a powerful moment; one that inspired joy in the midst of sorrow, life in the midst of death.

Chapter 38

SUSPICIOUS MINDS

I was about to step forward to share a memory about Mama but Sister Sally Streisand beat me to the punch. She knew Mama many years back when Dad first moved to Conundrum County. Sally and Mama shared a special bond created by a shared love for Elvis Presley. They had even attended an Elvis concert together where they both bumped into Priscilla. Meeting the king was one thing but meeting the wife of the king made it all the more special.

I'll never forget the Sunday that they both broke out into a popular Elvis song to try and ease some tension that had formed among the leadership board over missing money from the Sunday school. Someone had taken all the quarters out of the small church banks placed in each of the eight classrooms. Under suspicion were all the teenage kids with Burt and me as prime suspects. Gossiping had raged fiercely for several months with slanderous tongues wagging maliciously.

Well Sister Sally and Mama did something about it. They

felt the king had a thing or two to say about what was going on. I'll never forget the Sunday during worship when Dad became pale as the moon on a starry night when Sally began crooning Suspicious Minds with her husband Rhett accompanying on guitar strumming in perfect rhythm to the snappy tune. *We can't go on together with suspicious minds and we can't build our dreams on suspicious minds.*

And then Mama popped up from the pew joining Sally in the chorus while making her way upfront shaking and gyrating like Elvis. I thought Dad would have a heart attack on the spot.

The hysterical memory evoked a wry grin as I glanced over at Burt who returned my gaze wearing an uneasy look of guilt on his face. Poor Dad. He tried so hard to keep us all in check but the harder he tried the more rebellious we became. Mama was just so much more fun-spirited than Dad that it was almost comical to watch the two pulling in opposite directions almost naturally so. Eventually Dad just gave up the fight but only after many memorable "Dear God Annabelle" moments.

Dad squirmed a little in his seat as Sister Sally began singing the all-too-familiar tune evoking an unpleasant memory for him. But for the rest of us it was a "you go Mama" moment. I leaned over and whispered to Dad, "This one is on me." He began to loosen up a bit and simply said,

"I figured."

Laughter and clapping began spreading around the chapel. I knew that Mama would rather have Sister Sally sing an Elvis tune than one of the dreadfully, depressing hymns always sung at church funerals. I also knew that I would have some answering to do once the memorial service was over as it was becoming clearer to Dad with each passing moment that I had commandeered the order of celebration.

When Sister Sally sat down Millie stood up and gave her a thunderous applause that lingered noticeably so after the rest of us had stopped clapping. It was readily apparent that Millie had taken a few more nips from her flask during the soulful rendition of the Elvis classic. She then began making her way to the front. *This is only going to get better*, I thought glancing over at Joelle who was getting more tickled by the minute.

Chapter 39

"BLESS YOUR HEART"

Millie made her way to the front of the chapel with a swagger in her stride and a blue suede purse at her side. She handled her drink well and carried herself in a decorous way. Her voice quivered as she recounted how Mama helped her during a dark period of her life.

"Annabelle was a dear friend and a companion of the heart," Millie began becoming misty-eyed. Dad turned his gaze away from the floor an exception from his normal style of looking down when someone was talking. His undivided attention was now focused on Millie who he believed was nothing more than an uncouth drunk. But Dad had never taken the time to really get to know Millie like Mama did. And it became disturbingly apparent to him as she began to recount the life-altering impact Mama had made on her life.

"When my dear Bob along with our son Joey died in a plane crash nearly thirty years ago, it was Annabelle who was my compass home. Along with Bob and Joey, I lost faith in myself, God, and in life. I was overrun by darkness and grief and lost my will to live and would've ended it if not for Annabelle."

Millie took a brief moment to collect her composure as bittersweet emotions caused the words to stick in her throat. Tissues were rising to faces around the chapel like flags of surrender as grieving emotions were released with sweet abandon. Even Dad raised his hand to wipe away a tear sliding down his right cheek. I always thought that Dad suffered from Alexithymia but now discovered otherwise. It was a rare moment to witness Dad expressing empathy for a woman he had resented and detested for so long. It was a good moment.

Millie continued by saying, "Annabelle didn't get on a soap box and preach or tell me that I needed Jesus. And thank God she didn't tell me that Bob and Joey were in a better place because I probably would've vomited all over her." Nervous laughter was heard around the chapel mainly because of Burt and many others who had spoken the all-too-common statement earlier to family members.

"No, Annabelle was a constant companion unafraid to sit with me in the tomb of my grief. She listened and endured my emotional madness as only a true friend would or could. Slowly in time with the help of Annabelle and a little nip of JB's finest, I made my way out of the darkness back to the light. And I give thanks to God above for Annabelle, one of his brightest angels."

With her dark Sicilian eyes, Millie looked over at Burt adding, "Bless your heart young man. You needn't worry about the fate of your Mama's soul. You had only but ask and I would've told you the state of her soul. If ever a blessed soul entered Heaven's glory you can bet it was your Mama's. Besides, she always told me that part of her fringe benefits of being married to a preacher was guaranteed absolution." Everyone including Burt and Dad erupted in laughter.

I never viewed Millie the same again after that day. There were some things that Mama kept to herself and didn't tell the rest of us like those times when she left us with Dad and disappeared hours on end. It was during those times that Mama was serving as an angel of mercy to people like Millie who needed a comforting and reassuring presence. *Mama personified God's love*, I thought, wiping a tear away from my cheek. Millie made her way back to her seat leaving us awash in a sea of Mama's love.

Chapter 40

ANNABELLE'S SWEETHEART YEARS

After Millie sat down, Arlene rose and made her way to the front. She too carried with her a blue suede purse that looked just like Mama's. *Interesting*, I thought. Arlene and Mama had been friends since way back in high school. There was definitely history shared between the two. Just how much history we were all about to find out.

Arlene moved pretty well for a woman in her twilight years. She reminded me of Olive Oyl, the girlfriend of Popeye. Every bit of 5 feet 10 inches tall, Arlene walked upright down the chapel aisle almost as if she were on a fashion runway. She exuded a confidence that snapped you to attention. Her hair was cut short around the shoulders and dyed black with gray highlights. She had a dignified swag and kept her head held high not once looking down as she stepped to the front.

Turning to address us all, Arlene opened with a stunner, "Annabelle chased boys during her high school years." Dad suddenly flinched and was about to stand up when I pulled a

Joelle and placed a firm hand on his left knee physically holding him to the pew. He cleared his throat in agitation and was about to say something when Arlene continued, "Being Annabelle was a looker and all, she wouldn't tolerate any inappropriate nonsense from boys who were overly eager to become her steady. She'd chase em' and shoo em' off quicker than a toad frog could jump from one lily pad to the next. 'Dumb as a box of rocks,' she'd say. Annabelle certainly had a way of makin' em' scurry like chickens in a hen house."

Cackles and guffaws erupted around the chapel as Dad joined the levity of the moment releasing his pent up anxiety like air escaping a balloon. Even Elvis let out a woof and a brief, throaty howl. Jett egged him on, "Whistle Dixie old boy!"

Arlene was just getting warmed up as she fed off the crowd's responsiveness. "I do believe the movie Grease was inspired by Annabelle and her high school flame Hurley." No she didn't, I thought with a wince. Hurley has always been a sore subject with Dad and one we all knew better than to bring up. Those two had history and not of the celebratory kind. More like that of Cowboys and Indians. I mean, when you look up friction in the dictionary you'd find Dad and Hurley popping up as synonyms.

"I know it's probably not appropriate to bring up Annabelle's prior love interests at her memorial service especially with the green-eyed monster in the room," Arlene said while cutting her eyes over at Dad. "But life is life and Hurley was a big part of Annabelle's sweetheart years. I for one thought they would go the distance and I'm not just talking about crossing home plate either." Some snickers and uneasy laughter broke out in the chapel and died just as quickly.

Arlene pulled out a tissue from her blue suede purse and lightly touched her eyes with it. "Annabelle taught me a lot about love. And it's because of her good sense that I found me a loving man and kept him close to my side for nearly forty years until the good Lord finally took him home."

Arlene continued to hold us in rapt attention when she shared another kernel of Mama's word of advice to men about courting women, "'If you ain't right at the lip then don't expect to be tight with her at the hip.' Annabelle certainly didn't mince any words with her girlie girls. And she didn't mince any words with me either. I learned from her that a man who is worth his salt will speak to you respectively, kindly, and endearingly. And that was the code I lived by when it came to men. I learned that from Annabelle. That was the kind of woman she was. And the kind of woman that I always strived to be like. May she forever rest in peace."

Being a Catholic, Arlene finished by crossing herself

before returning to her seat. We all sort of sat there in stunned silence more from wondering how Dad was taking her comments than anything else. But before we had time to think long on the matter another brazen soul made her way to the front.

Chapter 41

MOODY BLUE

The next person to come forward was none other than Maisie, a southern belle if there ever was one from Mama's hometown of Charleston, South Carolina. Now quite the character Maisie was a highfalutin Charlestonian who had a swag in her gait with a colorful personality to back it up. Mama referred to Maisie as "Moody Blue" because she could go from sunshine to thunder and lightning in a blink of an eye.

Dad bristled when she strutted by with her blue suede purse in tow and an audible "humph" as she made her way to the front. *What is up with the blue suede purses?* I thought curiously. *More than a mere coincidence, there is clearly more to this oddity than meets the eye.* My sleuth inclinations were interrupted by Maisie's words.

"Mark Twain once said, 'I don't give a damn for a man that can only spell a word one way.'" Folks cringed in the chapel upon hearing the cuss word as if lightning from on high would strike at any moment. But Maisie was fearless not missing a beat as she continued to share her fond thoughts of Mama.

"Well that was the sort of attitude that Annabelle took while living her life. Bawn and bred in the jewel bed of our great nation, every bit a child of the South, and one of Chawleston's golden gals, Annabelle distinguished herself as a thoroughbred among women," Maisie said with a strong Southern drawl.

"I had the privilege of growing up with Annabelle and found her to be a delightful soul filled with rainbows and honeysuckles. She dreamed sweetly and had the most magical play world one could ever experience. Once I entered I discovered late in life I never really left it. You see Annabelle was one of those rare southern belles that once she envisioned something she actually made you believe that it was real. In all my bawn days, I haven't seen such imagination and creativity like I witnessed in her."

Maisie took a moment to remove a tissue from her blue suede purse and gently patted the moisture away from her eye. "I'll never forget once when I went with Annabelle and a few other lady friends to see the king in concert. It was a spiritual moment that brought all of us to our knees in such a memorable way. I don't know who gyrated more, Elvis or Annabelle but let me tell you one thing, hips don't lie and

Annabelle's certainly didn't."

A nervous bray of laughter was heard around the chapel but then fell abruptly silent. Mustering all the restraint he could, Dad was twitching and twerking like Mount Vesuvius about to erupt raining fire and ash down on Maisie's Pompeii.

I thought Maisie was finished speaking but she wasn't. Slumping in the pew, I wanted to crawl under to escape before Maisie lit fire to Dad's short fuse. Bracing for the inevitable, I knew she had Dad in her crosshairs for there was no love lost between those two. I was beginning to think she and Arlene had conspired together with what they would say because it was looking more like a tag team effort by the minute.

"Word has it that Annabelle's remains are to be buried here in Conundrum. Well the soil is not rich enough for her ashes," Maisie said while cutting her eyes over at Dad. "Just sayin'." The meaning was not lost on Dad. I could visibly see the Devil take possession as his face turned several shades of red quicker than Charleston's no-see-ums can swarm around you on a hot summer's day.

I reached over and stayed Dad's knee holding him fast to the pew bench as Maisie strolled back to her seat as the smell of Chanel No 5 was wafting in her wake leaving us with an aromatic scent that was Mama's fragrance of choice. I believe it was the familiar scent that restored calm to Dad's boiling stew as his thoughts returned to Mama.

Knowing something had to be done and done in short fashion to quail any further digs at Dad, I mustered the necessary gumption and stood to my feet. It was time that I took action and brought some relief to Dad before he had a coronary.

Chapter 42

THAT'S ALRIGHT MAMA

Quickly I jumped up before one of Mama's lady friends beat me to the punch. Sure enough there was Trudy making her way across a pew bench but upon noticing that I was standing front and center she quietly sat down proffering a reassuring smile as she did so. Looking around the room, I sensed a stirring of Mama's spirit. So many lives touched by her life created a palpable awareness of her presence.

How do you speak about someone who has meant so much to you? I briefly deliberated amidst the silence and gave voice to the first thing that came to mind. "I'm starting to believe that Elvis is not dead," eliciting a cacophony of laughs around the room. Glancing to each in turn I said, "Thank you Maisie, Sally, Arlene, and Millie for reminding us of what a great woman Mama was. She certainly had a way of drawing colorful personalities to her inner circle." More chuckles rippled around the chapel as I beamed appreciatively at Mama's closest admirers.

"Mama was a lady that you could count on to say and do

what was in her heart. But Mama also could talk a cat out of a tree. The good Lord broke the mold when he made Mama; one of a kind and forever a shining star in the heavens above. She could be most convincing to even the most contrary of souls."

"I remember on more than one occasion when Mama would pull us kids aside and tell it like it was. And she recognized smack when she heard it as well as slack when she saw it. Mama possessed a keen sense for fairness. She'd make Dad walk the line when she felt there was preferable treatment being shown to one child over the other." Dad fidgeted in the pew.

"On one occasion Dad bought Burt a bike but neglected to buy me one. There were times I felt that Dad had forgotten he had another son. I can still hear Mama saying to Dad, 'Now you know good and well that dog won't hunt' reminding him that if you're going to do something for one son you had better do it for the other one as well. Mama was the great equalizer."

It was hard to stand up front and speak from the heart when most of my memories were about Mama coming to my aid when I was a small tike. I also had other thoughts that I knew better than give utterance because of possible backlash from Dad. But suffice it to say I had on more than one occasion come to Mama's rescue as well and Dad knew it full well. But those memories would go with me to the grave and were better left unsaid.

"Mama was the absolute best. She loved us kids, loved her friends, loved her animals, and loved her husband. There was nothing she wouldn't do for you if there was a genuine need that needed to be met. That was the kind of person she was. She'd love you back in the saddle and send you galloping on your way."

"Mama nurtured my imagination and encouraged wide-eyed dreams. If not for her, I would've never followed through on the patent for a new line of men's wear designed for 'man boobs' and 'barrel bellies'." Laughter was heard around the room.

"I've made a mint off that clothing patent and I owe it all to Mama's encouragement. That was Mama for you – big encouragement for big dreams. When I struggled and endured some let downs in life she would take my hand and say, 'Hackett, how can I help make it better?' I would just smile and say, 'That's alright Mama.' She always loved the endearing way I made Elvis' first hit my response to her loving overtures."

Turning to look at Mama's picture on the altar next to the wooden urn, I said, "Mama, you will always be the rainbow I look for in the midst of the storms of life. I'll miss and love you always." A swirl of emotions, I finished and returned to my seat. Life just didn't feel the same without Mama in it. I couldn't imagine a future that didn't include her. Death sucks. Plain and simple.

Chapter 43

MAMA'S BLUE SUEDE PURSE

After returning to my seat, Joelle stood and made her way to the front with a blue suede purse in her hands. I recognized it. It was Mama's. Where did she find it? I wondered. The woman never ceased to amaze me. She certainly had my rapt attention as well as Dad's sitting next to me. Wasting no time, Joelle dove right in.

"I've known Annabelle for nearly thirty years now. But one of my fondest memories was when we first met. I was sitting on the front porch swing at her home in Charleston with Hackett. Well, on that fateful day Hackett got the urge to reach over and attempt to unbutton my top right then and there on his Mama's porch swing. His Mama wasn't having any of it. Speaking through the slightly cracked window I still remember her words as vividly as I do Hackett's reaction to them. 'Hackett, that ain't fitting.' That boy leapt up off that swing so fast you'd thunk a household of frogs had taken up residence inside them pants he was a wearing. All embarrassed and flustered Hackett tried to recover, 'Mama, I was just trying to swipe a bee away from her chest.' His Mama wasn't buying the nonsense he was trying to sell."

Guffaws were heard around the chapel as Joelle was just starting to get warmed up. She owned the floor and commanded everyone's attention. Feeling an anxiety attack coming on, I feared what she was going to say next. Dad was taking devilish delight in what she was saying since the mud being slapped around was now directed my way.

In rare form Joelle continued, "I can still hear Annabelle's response to Hackett, 'You think I was born on crazy creek? Now get your hands away from where they don't belong.' After a few moments she came outside with some sweet tea and we just hit it off from the get go. A mother who can jerk a knot in her baby boy, especially one who chews his own tobacco, without so much as lifting a hand is a woman worth her weight in gold."

Joelle took the blue suede purse that she was holding in her hand and laid it on the altar next to Mama's urn. She just stood there with her back to us all and lingered for what seemed a few awkward moments. I couldn't help but wonder what was going through her mind but something told me that she was about to let us in on the mystery. And she did.

"Oh, how Annabelle loved her some Elvis."

"Amen!" Millie said taking a quick hit from her flask.

"Don't you know it," Sister Sally injected from the front

where she was sitting on the piano bench. I thought she was going to break out into another Elvis favorite of Mama's but she yielded the floor to Joelle's musings.

"And I'll never forget when Elvis got loose in the church and Annabelle who came running to rescue him from the brooms, pitchforks, and altar paraments. Elvis had picked up on a scent of some roast beef from the church cover dish and took a short cut through the sanctuary interrupting the church ladies who were praying in fervent fashion. Inspired to follow suit, Elvis began doing some praying of his own as he stopped in their midst and began howling right in front of the picture of Jesus. The ladies who worked so hard to keep everything so prim and proper in the hallowed space thought one of the hounds of hell had escaped the fiery pit. Oh my, what a fit they had trying to put their saintly hands on that sinful dog. Annabelle laughed hysterically while trying to appreciate the serious offense Elvis had committed in the eyes of the church ladies. Annabelle and Elvis certainly made life delightful and adventurous. What a team they were but that is a tale for another time." Elvis gave out another short howl.

The folks around the chapel as well as Elvis were tracking with Joelle hanging on every word she said. I began wondering how I could've missed some of the more interesting happenings in Mama's life. I thought about how wrapped up in my own life I had been after moving out of the home as an adult missing out on some of the special moments that made Mama's life so colorful. Joelle distracted my thoughts as she lifted Mama's blue suede purse in the air continuing.

"When Annabelle carried her blue suede purse on special occasions it was her way of serving notice to others and especially the vipers in the church that certain things were off limits to gossip, criticism and slander, like her family. Her blue suede purse was a symbol representing a protective love for her family and closest friends. And when she carried it on her person it was a visible reminder that you had better not mess with her clan. Just like in the song, 'don't step on my blue suede shoes.'"

Joelle finished by kissing endearingly, Mama's blue suede purse placing it ever so respectively back on the altar. She then returned to her seat sitting down next to me. I had never been more proud of her than I was in that moment feeling nothing but a hunk, a hunk of burning love.

Chapter 44

THE BLUE SUEDE PURSES

Bishop JD was about to step to the podium when Sister Sally began putting fingers to keys as the piano came to life with a peppy rendition of the Elvis classic, Blue Suede Shoes. And then ten ladies from out of the pews began dancing their way to the front with Joelle joining them. Momentarily stunned with amusement, I then did what felt natural and started clapping in time with the music.

Sally began belting out the words to *Blue Suede Shoes*, and the ladies sang out putting particular emphasis on the word purses replacing the word shoes in the chorus. I never seen the mature in years get so excited and expressive waving their blue suede purses around in the air. Odd but rather delightful to see and hear. Knowing Mama, it was probably some kind of secret ladies society anthem.

Those southern cats sure did know how to move their bodies which were clearly north of the younger years. But WOW! What they lacked in youth they more than made up for in heart.

Bishop JD and Rev. Mario glanced at each other with apprehension on their faces. They were clearly beside themselves with how to handle the unscripted song and dance number by Mama's lady friends who were readily gyrating and waving their blue suede purses around as if they had just won a national bingo contest. Bishop JD looked to Dad who was shocked and baffled by the turn of events.

Trudy, another dear friend of Mama's from Charleston broke out into her own thing with an eye popping, jaw dropping throw down of the 1920's dance, "Doin' the Charleston". At this point the chapel was beginning to look and feel like a Charleston speakeasy with lots of hootin' and a hollerin'.

The memorial service was quickly getting out of control. Squiditch found his way back into the room and leapt up onto the altar and spread his arms wide while swaying side to side. Elvis let out a woof and short howl as he jumped down off the pew careening right into the back of Bishop JD who was trying to catch Squiditch. Knees buckling from behind, the Bishop hit the floor as the communion cups and remaining Jim Beam *Devil's Cut* came flowing down on him like some kind of baptism in whiskey. It was a "Sweet Jesus" moment for the Bishop.

Dad seemed to just give himself over to the mayhem as he surprisingly loosened up with a grin while starting to bob his head up and down to the music. I glanced over at the kids who were at this point standing in the pews just as happy, slappy as they could be.

Others who were unsure how to respond glanced my way looking for some kind of green light from the family to join in so I rose to my feet and started singing right along. Well that just unleashed a ruckus of a different sort. Folks followed suit as a myriad of feet joined the blue suede purses in a good old southern, foot stompin' hoedown. Sister Sally's husband pulled out his violin and began playing with fervent skill and passion. I knew that Mama's spirit had ascended in that chapel as surely as the Holy Ghost descended like a dove upon Jesus at his baptism.

Burt and his clan appeared horrified as if the Devil went down to Conundrum and took up residence in the chapel of the funeral home. They were beside themselves in confusion waiting for the Archangel Michael himself to show up and cast out the demonic spirits. But the for the rest of us, we knew that if he did appear, old Michael himself would join the blue suede purses upfront and dance in celebration of Mama's life.

At least for a few moments all was well in the universe as we all danced, laughed, and comingled stories and bodies turning the chapel into something more like a Footloose movie set than a setting for a memorial service. At this point the ministers were swaying almost enthusiastically with Bishop JD taking another shot from a remaining communion cup.

Maisie danced over and gave Dad a bump with her rump holding her hand out for him to do a dose doe with her. Dad hesitated but relented and gave Maisie a twirl or two. Mama's blue suede purse with silver accents appeared to sparkle in the light of it all. Mama would not have had it any other way.

Chapter 45

MEMORIES

The nostalgic moments inspired by all the testimonies stirred the heart and provided a welcome respite from the grief that weighed heavily on the soul. The memories stirred by the remembrances shared elicited a strong desire to go back and relive and re-experience each and every moment with Mama; to cherish even more those moments that I took for granted the first time around.

The stark reality is that we don't get a second chance to go back. We have only now and the next moment and if we're lucky maybe even a tomorrow to live and experience with loved ones. *Why is it that we often only grasp the gravity of this reality when it's too late?* I thought. But it wasn't just the moments that I experienced with Mama that tugged at my heart but rather the moments that I failed to seize that makes the grieving all the more sullen.

Bishop JD and Rev. Mario concluded the memorial service with a reading from Revelation promising a new heaven and a new earth. True to their ritual it was nonetheless a benign effort to leave us with a dash of hope in coping with Mama's death. But I wasn't interested in a new heaven and new earth. Big love, big smiles, and big support from Mama made Heaven a place on earth. Without her in it life would be a little less extraordinary.

A mixture of smiles and tears were on the faces of many as everyone recessed out of the chapel heading for vehicles to attend the graveside service at the Historic Conundrum County Cemetery. Joelle quickly walked over to the altar and grabbed Mama's blue suede purse and jumped back in line behind me as we walked down the aisle.

Stepping outside pure sunshine greeted us in dazzling splendor. A peace flooded my soul as I felt Mama's spirit bathing us in exquisite light that had never before felt so potent as it did that day. Joelle and the kids climbed into our Dodge Ram. Waiting for everyone to get into their vehicles I turned the radio on and Elvis' song, Memories began playing. I just chuckled as I looked over at Joelle and said, "What are the chances of that song coming on now?"

Bixie quickly interjected dispelling my mystical moment, "Dad, the song is coming from your iTunes playlist with ya-ya's favorite Elvis songs on it."

"Oh," I said. "Still, pretty cool for Memories to come on right now. I know Mama is listening." And without her typical, sarcastic style, Bixie replied, "Yes she is. Ya-ya is definitely vibing with you Dad."

We drove over to the Historic Conundrum County Cemetery following behind Dad and Mr. Buckley in the lead car. Elvis serenaded us with Memories as we all listened in reflective silence trailing along in the funeral procession at a snail's pace. It was a good ride as we became one with the music; memories taking flight on the wings of nostalgia.

Chapter 46

RETURN TO SENDER

Arriving at the Conundrum cemetery, we were greeted by a hodgepodge assortment of headstones and footstones. Mr. Buckley had successfully negotiated the only remaining plot from one of Conundrum's own blue bloods. It was big enough to bury two urns. Dad chose it for his and Mama's final resting place. I didn't much care for the setting, not for Mama, concurring with Maisie's sentiments, "The soil is not rich enough for her ashes." Mama's spirit would only be truly at rest when her ashes are buried back in Charleston.

Gathering beneath a tent, family and close friends were seated to witness the final rites. It was a somber moment but one made less painful knowing that Mama's ashes were not in the plain wooden urn sitting on the faux grass matt before us. Something about being among the tombstones made the wooden urn appear all the more cheap.

From under the tent canopy I gazed outside where my attention was drawn to ten ladies mature in years, all standing shoulder to shoulder, each holding a blue suede purse in hand displayed prominently in front of them. That was the revelatory moment in which I knew with certainty that Mama belonged to some type of mysterious secret ladies society. And it was the moment I made it my mission to uncover to what extent she was involved. My gut told me that Joelle knew more than she had let on. *Mama, what were you involved in?* I thought. *You sly devil you.*

Chuckling not realizing I was doing so, Joelle gave me one of her signature elbows to my right rib whereupon I winced and glanced down noticing a blue suede purse resting against her bosom. And it wasn't the one with Mama's ashes in it either. This one was a little less worn than Mama's. It was starting to eat me up inside and I could hardly focus on the seriously depressing final words the two ministers were taking turns reading and droning on about.

I had a hunch that Joelle was part of whatever it was that Mama had belonged to. My mind was racing now as I began to recount details about Mama's life that I had maybe overlooked. I found myself being drawn into a maze of mystery trying to crack the code that would unlock the secret of Mama's mysterious past; details about Mama that I was bound and determined to uncover.

Bishop JD finished the graveside rite reading from Ecclesiastes 12:7 NIV, "and the dust returns to the ground it came from, and the spirit returns to God who gave it." That's it! I thought incredulously. For some reason at that moment Elvis' song, *Return to Sender* came to mind. It was Mama's spirit speaking to me from beyond the grave.

This isn't a final rite, I mused to myself. For some this may have been the end of Mama's life but for me it was just the beginning. The beginning in that I was about to discover a part of her life I never knew existed. One filled with intrigue, mystery, and secrecy.

Glancing over at the blue suede purses, I received a knowing expression from Maisie as she smiled my way before turning to leave. I knew then and there that I had not heard nor seen the last of ole Maisie. Making a mental note of all that I had witnessed from these ladies of the blue suede purses, I was bound and determined to discover the extent to which Mama was a part of it all. And knowing Mama she was probably immersed as deep as you could get; maybe even lead dog.

Before I could turn to leave a furry friend jumped up on the heart-shaped wreath laying at the head of Mama's grave marker. Twitching and twerking his tail, Squiditch was nose up glancing my way. I proffered a smile and nodded my head in gratitude for his role in helping us switch Mama's ashes. I felt a kindred connection with that gray squirrel. And then a sadness came over me as I felt that it would be last time I would lay eyes on Squiditch. I hoped I was wrong.

Chapter 47

HAPPY HENRY'S CAFÉ

After the graveside service we all loaded up to go join Dad for a bite to eat at Happy Henry's Café. Opening the door to get in my truck, I was greeted by Elvis riding shotgun with an eager expression as if to say, "Let's roll!"

"What you doing old boy?" I asked while climbing up into the Dodge Ram. "Did you boot Bixie out?"

Jett pulled up in his Jeep Wrangler Unlimited with the top down and hollered, "Hey, Bixie's riding with me. See you at Henry's."

Louie piled in the front next to Elvis. "Well, alright," I said. "Let's go get something to eat." Elvis gave a short burst of a howl as I fired up the Dodge. Nudging the iTunes player on the dashboard with his right paw, Elvis selected Jailhouse Rock by the king. Hitting play, he just sort of casually looked my way with his doggy browns.

"You got your Mama's taste in music old boy," I said, patting his head. And then we were off and running, bopping to the king.

Happy Henry's is a quaint diner in the heart of town overlooking the Conundrum River. Burt and his clan didn't join us because they were hosting a barbeque at his house about forty-five minutes away. Now why Burt thought the family would gather at his house after the graveside service was beyond me. Lucinda and Phinn went home returning to their predictable, reclusive lives. But clearly Dad wasn't missing his daily routine of going to Happy Henry's and so it was just my clan accompanying him at his favorite diner.

The anxiety and tension so manifest in Dad over the past few days was noticeably absent from his demeanor. It was a rare pleasant side of Dad that we enjoyed during our meal. After a scrumptious spread consisting of a large seafood platter of shrimp, scallops, and oysters complimented with sweet, crunchy southern cole slaw and green beans we all just sat around and reflected on more highlights from our various experiences with Mama.

Elvis joined us inside sitting next to Jett on a high back bench. He was a frequent companion of Mama's whenever she went into town and Happy Henry's was no exception. Dad leaned in a little closer to the table as he took a sip from a glass of sweet, southern-style tea. "Your Mama possessed a mind of her own. There's no doubt about that," Dad said wearing an amused expression on his face. He looked at Joelle with a curious admiration in his eyes. "You're a gifted speaker Joelle. Your words come from the heart and put a spark in the soul."

"Why, thank you Theo. Annabelle was an inspiration to us all," Joelle said appreciatively in response to the flattering compliment.

Dad took another draught from his tea glass and continued reflecting about Joelle's words about Mama during the memorial service, "Annabelle was a great fan of Elvis Presley. I often wondered why on certain occasions she chose to take her blue suede purse when she went off to visit with friends. I just thought it was a stylistic choice and never made the connection with Elvis' song, Blue Suede Shoes. Your words were certainly meaningful as well as inspiring to so many at Annabelle's memorial service."

"It was definitely a one-of-a-kind memorial service that is for sure," I said shaking my head, chuckling at the memory. "Joelle's words lit a fire under Mama's lady friends turning the memorial service into a tour de force."

"Annabelle was every bit of what I said and more," Joelle said ardently. "A great woman whose free spirit equaled her sense of adventure."

Dad just took another sip of tea as he thoughtfully gazed in Joelle's direction as if deciphering the meaning behind her words. Dad could go from warm sunshine to a blistering blizzard in a fraction of a second but he had a special kind of affection for Joelle that consisted of respect and admiration.

Their relationship was able to kindle due in large part to Joelle's uncanny knack for winning folks over by knowing when to speak and when to listen. "Much can be learned about a person by listening more and speaking less," is Joelle's philosophy and how she found her way into Dad's heart. Joelle is as wise as she is discerning when it comes to Dad. And it has made all the difference in their relationship.

After our meal we all walked out with Dad to say goodbye before heading back to Charleston. A tear ran down Dad's cheek as we exchanged hugs. It was readily apparent that he was grieving and now that the memorial service was behind him, he was able to let go and allow himself to grieve more freely.

I pulled Dad aside for a private moment. "Would you like for us to keep Elvis for a bit, while you handle Mama's legal matters?"

"That would be most helpful. Elvis is grieving in his own way and without Mama around, he may need all of you more than me right now."

"No worries. We'll take good care of him and will see you again soon."

"We love you," Dad said inferring Mama's love as well. It was rare that Dad said those words making it all the more special. I watched Dad turn and walk across the street to his navy blue Prius. I couldn't help but wonder how much longer he would be with us. It was just a thought but one that elicited a sadness within. With Mama gone life would never be the same. Our family was feeling its mortality in a way that we hadn't before.

We all piled into the Dodge Ram and strapped ourselves in with Louie and Elvis sharing a seatbelt. Turning on the ignition, I cranked up another one of Mama's Elvis favorites, *Promised Land.*

Looking down at Mama's blue suede purse resting on the floorboard by Joelle's left leg, loving memories began to settle over me. One in particular was when Mama came walking out of the house when I was but a teen, with her blue suede purse in tow. Looking back at me before getting into her car she said, "I love you, Hackett."

"I love you too, Mama."

It was a good memory.

Chapter 48

LEAVING CONUNDRUM

Crossing the Conundrum County line on our way back to Charleston we saw a raccoon perched on a pier cap at the beginning of the Conundrum River Bridge. The raccoon was standing on his hind legs giving us a salute with his right paw as we approached. Wearing what appeared to be a big, ole grin across his bandit face with whiskers a twitching, the raccoon did a flip in the air landing a perfect "stick" on the pier cap.

Louie scrambled to get his window down and was half hanging out when he yelled back, "Hey Dad, look at the raccoon!" We all waved enthusiastically as we raced on by. Gazing into the rearview mirror, my thoughts turned to Rally. A strong sense came over me that I hadn't seen the last of him. Some things you just know in the core of your being.

Strangely enough, I was bummed to be leaving old Conundrum. Those few magical days had left an indelible mark on my soul. The enchanting experience meeting Rally and other Great Spirits who shared a special connection with

Mama helped to give me an alternate perspective about life, death, and the great beyond. And old Conundrum County played a special part as the staging ground for bringing together Mama's finest, giving her a fitting send off.

Looking in the rearview mirror was like seeing a part of Mama's life drift further away. It was time to pep us all up a bit so I selected *Life is a Highway* by Rascal Flatts from my iTunes playlist turning it up. Elvis' ears were bopping to the tune as everyone joined in for a sing along.

I couldn't help but think that life really is a highway and along the way one meets colorful characters that contribute to your story. Colorful characters such as Rally, Squiditch, Buckminister, Seagle, and Elvis, all who loved Mama as much as any of us. Mama loved animals there was no disputing that. But what I discovered during my efforts to switch Mama's ashes was how much the animals loved her back.

The animal kind cherished Mama as much as any human ever had. I couldn't help but think about the scripture verse in 1 John 4:8 NIV that states, "…God is love." Well another thought flitted across my mind, "Animals are love." They embody God's love as much if not more so than any human ever had.

Memories worth remembering are those special moments shared with love ones that are forever captured by the mind's eye and stored in the heart. Now more than ever before, each memory of Mama is a cherished experience that will keep her spirit alive in my heart always. By looking back I find inspiration to move forward into a future made bright by memories of Mama who taught us to live adventurously, love generously, and laugh heartily.

I began reflecting upon the experiences I shared with Mama from a new perspective while settling into the drive home drifting off to that place of happy thoughts.

Chapter 49

ROADSIDE DUNNY

We were well on our way back to Charleston when it hit us all at once. My palms started getting clammy and sweat was breaking out profusely on my forehead. *You've got to be kidding me*, I thought. I cast a sickly eye Joelle's way and she was also sweating profusely while turning fifty shades of green. The kids with the exception of Bixie who hadn't eaten any seafood at Happy Henry's, were beginning to complain of stomach cramps. It was a nightmare in the making on I-95 South.

Riding along I anxiously scanned for an upcoming exit but as always, there's never an exit when you need one. We weren't anywhere close to an exit that would take us to a restroom facility. I began to experience a flashback of a trip that Joelle and I took years earlier in the bush, the Australian outback bush that is. We were riding along at the time amid a bus load of other tourists and I was in a worse way needing to use a restroom.

The tour guide noticed the uncomfortable look on my face

and asked, "You need to use a dunny?"

"Huh?" I replied.

"A dunny?" Picking up on my ignorance of Australian slang he clarified, "Do you need to use a toilet?"

"Oh. Yes," I replied somewhat embarrassed.

To make matters even more embarrassing, the guide instructed the bus driver to pull over so that I could go use the au natural dunny among the outback. Thoroughly embarrassed I struck out looking for a bush to hide behind out of sight of the bus. And then I couldn't release bodily fluids with the thought racing through my mind that EVERYONE back on the bus was ever aware that I was nearly waist deep in Australian lemon-scented foliage called "Bottle-Brush" trying to relieve myself. Maybe it was also the scent of lemons that shut me down but I just kind of stood out in that field of embarrassment long enough so that everyone would think I had done my business. It was a long trip back to Sydney, let me tell you.

I was stirred from the less than pleasant memory by Joelle's urgent directive, "You need to pull over now!" Not wasting anytime arguing with her, I immediately complied pulling off the interstate. Bixie was cackling and feigned compassion by asking, "You guys need some tp?"

"No time," I replied hurriedly feeling the rumblings in my bowels like a volcano stirring to life. Doors opened simultaneously as all of us except Bixie, jumped out of the truck and in short time made our way to a fence that stood nearly six feet tall. "Great," I said. In the worst kind of way, I immediately began scanning the width of the fence running parallel along the interstate. There was nowhere to go but up and over.

Grabbing Louie, I quickly heaved him up where he fastened to the metal fencing and scaled it effortlessly as if he were Spider-Man. The girls followed suit making short work of the climb and were off and running on the other side following after Louie into the dense woods beyond. Joelle and I heard several vehicle horns as we were struggling to climb the fence. But it was one of those desperate moments in life when you could care less about what others were thinking because you are so focused on relieving your misery.

I must've mooned several vehicles trying to get my pants down as I breached the tree line along the interstate. Stumbling over my pants, I somersaulted rolling up on my back feet at which time I commenced a refreshing discharge of diarrhea that hit the ground like rapid fire from a Gatling gun. I had never been so physically relieved as I was in that moment. Happy to jettison every last vestige of food that I had eaten at Happy Henry's, I was one ecstatic camper.

Making our way back to the truck after scaling the fence, we all just acted normal like, as if we had been on a family adventure exploring the wild along the interstate. It was a memorable moment for sure.

Bixie greeted us with her typical mocking cackle, "Feel better? What did you wipe with?"

"Funny," I said, getting into the truck. "Use your imagination." I turned the ignition and cranked up Elvis', *A Little Less Conversation*, and we were on our way home.

Chapter 50

HOME SWEET HOME

We pulled up into the driveway of our beach home on Sullivan's Island, a quaint island town providing stunning views of the Charleston harbor. The kids along with Elvis pulling up the rear, wasted no time clambering out of the truck and running inside the house to change and hit the beach. Betty Lou, who had been keeping Queen Bean, our Chihuahua, opened the door giving the kids a hearty hug as they entered.

Elvis strolled lazily up to the front porch where his appraising eyes were transfixed by the most beautiful creature he had ever seen of the female animal kind. Standing on all fours with her white tail curled back and pointy ears erect was none other than the Belle of the South, our precious and precocious, Queen Bean.

Elvis felt a hot flush spread out from his vitals. It was love at first sight. Queen Bean instantaneously became the object of his desires and fantasies as Elvis' mind drifted back to the cab of the Dodge Ram envisioning himself sitting behind the wheel with Queen Bean snuggled up against him. Nudging the iTunes player on the dashboard with his right paw and selecting Kid Rock's, *Johnny Cash*, Elvis hit play.

Gazing longingly down at his lover with his doggy browns, Elvis felt complete in her eyes. Queen Bean returned his gaze with a yip, yip, and a yap. *Oh, you want a drink*, Elvis said, moving his jaws at the thought. Getting out of the truck, Elvis followed behind Queen Bean as words from the song flowed through his mind, *I like the way you shake and work it. Ten out of ten, baby you're perfect.*

Stepping up and onto the wrap around porch they walked along stopping in front of attached doggy bowls overlooking a gorgeous apricot sun setting in the distance. Hackett came over and poured bourbon in Elvis' bowl and a little bit of merlot in Queen Bean's. Elvis lapped slowly mesmerized by how Queen Bean's tongue teasingly lapped at the wine. She looked up at him with another yip, yip, and a yap stirring him back to reality. Shaking his head, Elvis realized he was standing on the porch in a daze. He had been fantasizing again.

Playing hard to get, Queen Bean with her Chihuahua sass, scuttled off along the wraparound porch. Quickly shaking off the stimulating feelings from his fantasy, Elvis chased off in hot pursuit.

"I think Elvis has got an achy breaky heart," I said to

Joelle watching him make double time trying to catch up to the Queen Bean. Never had it felt so good to be back home. Our harbor front property had been in the family for generations with ease of access to the beach. Looking down at Mama's blue suede purse, I felt a sense of relief that she would finally be laid to rest at her home in Charleston. Joelle reached over and squeezed my hand as if reading my thoughts. I was fortunate to have a sugar love like Joelle. Mama often reminded me of that fact saying, "You wouldn't be any richer if you had picked the winning numbers for the lottery." And she was right.

Charleston and Mama went together like milk and honey. One of my fondest memories of Mama was sitting by the fireplace while listening to her tell some interesting yarns about her years growing up in Charleston. Some of these tales I once thought were embellished but after the events of the past few days, I was starting to believe most, if not all, were actually factual.

There were many facets to Mama's life that I was just discovering. Far from a one dimensional woman, Mama was like a brilliant cut diamond with many interesting angles revealing aspects of her life that would absolutely dazzle in the light of revelation. Mama's fascinating life was filled with intrigue, drama, and adventure.

Sometimes I wondered why Mama followed Dad into the

ministry all those years ago. She had everything in Charleston. I can only surmise that love is indeed, the greatest mystery of all.

But Mama's love had its limitations when it came to Dad and his desire for her to sever all ties with Charleston. Dad at one time wanted to sell the Sullivan's Island beach home that had been passed down to Mama but she would have none of it. It's not that Dad didn't like Charleston, he was just threatened by anything that held Mama's greater affection. So, I stepped in and bought the property from Mama which was a workable compromise. Dad initially resented me for buying the property but came to accept it. Mama would bring Elvis with her when she came to Charleston for a visit. Most of the time, Dad would come up with some church related excuse for not accompanying her.

Looking out the window of the truck at our saltbox home, I drifted off in thought contemplating the good times shared with Mama around the island. Joelle disturbed my reflections, "What's on your mind hon?"

"I was just thinking about Mama and Dad. They had such an interesting relationship always teetering between love and hate, peace and war. Such strong personalities and yet they held together all those years."

"Their relationship and marriage was a testament to a love that was stronger than their differences. You must admit, it was anything but bland and uneventful," Joelle said chuckling.

"I know, right?"

We shared a good laugh and then got out of the truck walking hand in hand to our home sweet home.

Chapter 51

MAMA AND THE SALT LIFE

Joelle and I rocked lazily on the porch watching the sun retreat below the rim of the world. Mama's old home was perfectly positioned on prime, waterfront property to maximize views of the sun rising over the Atlantic to the east and setting beyond the Charleston skyline off to the west. Enjoying the picturesque views, we rocked and sipped sweet tea from our Tumblers.

The kids were making sand castles on the beach as the flags waved in the breeze on Fort Sumter just across the way in the harbor. Sullivan's Island held some great childhood memories. Playing during summers on the beach, surf fishing with Mama, and taking in the ever-changing nautical vistas filled my childhood with enchanting experiences and memories. Those were the memories that I cherished now more than ever before keeping Mama's spirit alive inside of me.

The death of a loved one is a wakeup call to remember how fragile life is and that one must never take it for granted.

Mama's death taught me to cherish even more the moments shared with Joelle and the kids. For you never know when a moment shared with a family member may be the last moment you ever share with them again.

"Your Mama loved the salt life," Joelle said reflectively. "I'll never forget the time we were surf fishing on the beach together after Allie was born. Just beyond the seawall over there by Fort Moultrie at low tide she hooked a five foot Bonnethead shark. I thought your Mama was going to swim in after that fish. I've never seen such fight in a fisherwoman; so bound and determined to win against the fin. It was like your Mama's version of an angler fight club. It took nearly an hour for your Mama to reel that shark in but eventually she did just that. That's when I knew your Mama was not someone you wanted to scrap with. When she set her mind to something there was no stopping her."

"Yeah, and I remember you running inside with Allie swinging in your arms yelling, 'Annabelle caught Jaws!'" I laughed at the recollection as Joelle and I gazed over at that seawall.

I wished I had been there to have seen it, to have experienced it, but I also had numerous memories of competing with Mama for the catch of the day and then taking our bucket full of fish home to filet and cook. Mama made the salt life extra special. When he was in town, she'd drag Dad out of the house and onto the beach when given to one of his stupors derived from the harassing church life that often hounded him as a pastor. I can still hear Mama saying to him, "Theo, the salt air will do you some good." And it certainly did when Dad would let go and let Poseidon and Mama wield their soul-healing, salt life charm.

Joelle affectionately squeezed my hand and turned her head my way while leaning back on the rocker. "Hackett, we need to talk about where we're going to scatter your Mama's ashes here in Charleston. And there is also something else we need to discuss."

Glancing over at Joelle and the look on her face, my gut told me I would need something stronger than sweet tea in my Tumbler. Raising my finger in the air, I signaled for Joelle to pause for a moment. I jumped up and walked inside as my mind began to race with all kinds of crazy thoughts about what she was about to tell me. But I knew by the tone in her voice that the words to follow would probably shock the jock right out of me. I had an inkling that our lives were about to change. Of that I was certain.

Chapter 52

JOELLE'S REVELATION

Walking into the kitchen, I mixed myself a fruity concoction; my version of a Mai Tai. Taking a deep draught from the Tumbler and wincing as the spirits went down strong, I was now primed to hear just what Joelle had to discuss. Squeaky clean, I knew there was no dirty laundry to air. Well, at least the clothes on my back were clean because I hadn't had time to wash the others from the road trip. So something else was up.

After being married to Joelle for nearly thirty years, I'd learned to trust my gut and right now my gut was telling me to drink and to do so heartily.

Easing back out on the porch I caught the last light of day as the sun dipped beneath the horizon. Joelle had gotten up and was leaning against the porch rail. Breaking the awkward silence, I asked, "So, break it to me. What is this mystery you mean to unveil, sugar plum?"

"Oh sugar smacks, the mystery has everything to do with your history. I just want to let you in on it."

I was caught off guard. She had me at, "Oh".

Waiting a few moments as if collecting her thoughts and carefully considering her words Joelle continued, "The night we last saw your Mama after we had stepped out of the room. I had told you I was going to the restroom. Well I sort of lied. I actually went back to say one last goodbye to your Mama. When I walked into the room she was wearing the most divine smile on her face. It was a beatific moment and one that I will never forget for as long as the Good Lord above blesses me with the gift of life. When I walked over to your Mama's bedside, she reached out and took my hand in her own gently squeezing as she did so with a smile. She then removed her blue suede purse from beneath the bed sheet taking my hand and placing it on the purse before drifting off into a most peaceful sleep. In the purse was a note and a letter."

Joelle paused gauging my reaction. And then she let it rip, "Your Mama was the head of a secret ladies society called The Blue Suede Purses. And it was formed by your Mama who, as you know, was a devout fan of the king, Elvis Presley himself. The note inside the purse was her last will and testament for The Blue Suede Purses."

Joelle just let her words hang in the air as if dangling a tender morsel of sirloin in front of me. I knew she was wanting me to bite but my Mai Tai had already kicked in so I chose to play it cool.

"Oh, you look so cute when you're telling dirty secrets my little blue suede kitten. Meow, meow," I purred trying to best her at this mental game of cat and mouse. And daggone if I was going to be the mouse.

"Seriously, Hackett. Your Mama was the ONE who started what has now grown into a full-fledged, national secret society that rivals the likes of the Illuminati, the Knights Templar, and those Masons. Inspired by love for the king and his music this grass roots movement has been instrumental in shaping the hearts and lives of many as well as influencing the course of history. I don't know if you noticed or not but the memorial service ran rife with codespeak by members of The Blue Suede Purses who provided testimonials about your Mama."

Taking another sip from my Mai Tai, I just sort of eyed Joelle for a moment while processing the implications of her words. "You're serious, aren't you?" I asked restraining myself from busting out in a Yee-haw guffaw. But then I noticed that her eyes didn't blink nor did her face flinch. *Dang woman, you ARE serious*, I thought to myself incredulously.

"Well, aren't you going to say anything?" Joelle asked.

Speaking the first words that came to mind I responded, "You're the Devil in disguise!"

"Funny, Hackett," Joelle said while rolling her eyes. "Be

serious for once in your life. I had to tell you because not only did your Mama request that you bury her ashes on Sullivan's Island but also that a handful of her ashes are to be scattered on the grounds of Graceland in Memphis. It's a pledge that all members are beholden to have honored upon their death."

"Are you freaking kidding me?" I cried out. "Seriously? We are to spread some of Mama's ashes on Elvis' grave?"

"Yes. And that's not all. Your Mama has nominated that I replace her as the TCB. It's all right here in her letter," Joelle said holding it up in her hand. There's more but I can't read her last will and testament for the society until all of the ladies gather for the upcoming, sacred conclave at a specified location that your Mama has chosen.

"Seriously? You're referring to Elvis' 'Taking Care of Business' slogan symbolized by the lightning bolt?"

"Well, not exactly. TCB, as used by The Blue Suede Purses stands for The Chic Belle, the leader of the society."

Shaking my head, I was hardly believing what my ears were hearing. "Sounds like The Blue Suede Purses is nothing but a female version of the Memphis Mafia."

"Exactly," Joelle said with a malevolent grin breaking across her face. "Aren't you just a chip off the old block?"

All I could think to myself was, *Mama, what have you gotten Joelle entangled in?* I then took a long draught from my Mai Tai finishing it off in hopes of speeding up the effects of the mind-numbing elixir. Our lives were about to change. Glancing over, I noticed Elvis chillaxin' on the porch just a waggin' his tail with Queen Bean sitting at his side. "You're both probably TCB secret service agents," I said jokingly. They both suddenly lifted their heads with Elvis giving a hearty baying howl and Queen Bean a yip, yip, and a yap.

"Dear God, ya'll are!"

Chapter 52

MAMA'S NOTE

Joelle pulled out the note from inside the blue suede purse. She then handed it to me and said, "This one's for you."

My emotions began to churn as I held for a few silent moments the bi-folded note in my hand, realizing that I was holding Mama's last words written to me. Strolling off toward the beach I headed over to where the water was breaking across the shoreline feeling the misty spray on my bare feet. Joelle stayed back giving me alone time to process Mama's final words contained in the letter. Elvis walked alongside ever the faithful companion.

I inhaled deeply the salt air as I opened Mama's note and began to read.

My Dearest Hackett,

You've always been my pride and joy. From the moment the first thought of you entered my mind you lit an eternal flame in my soul.

You're my special sunshine that has always filled me with warmth inside. Though life has not always been easy for you, I've watched you prevail in the face of adversity. You possess a resilience that keeps you bouncing back stronger and more determined than ever before. You've always been there for me when I've needed you. Go easy on your father. He means well although he doesn't always communicate it effectively. He can be stubborn as you well know. But stubborn is as stubborn does. You just have to beat him at his own game. I know that in reading this letter you have or soon will lay my ashes to rest. PLEASE don't let your father bury my remains in the Historic Conundrum County Cemetery. Nothing against the blessed souls laid to rest there but you know that the memories of my heart are treasured moments along the salty shores of Sullivan's Island. Know that I will always love you, more dearly than life itself. Be good and kind to Joelle. She is also near and dear to my heart and a precious soul. Love those grandbabies always. And if a few furry friends of mine come a calling welcome and embrace them, as you would me. I love you!

Forever in my heart,
Mama

Closing the note, I just gazed out upon the expansive Atlantic while marinating in Mama's words, allowing them to season my soul with her love. She was the grand matriarch of our family and now she was gone. There was an emptiness inside that began aching for her presence. I couldn't believe she was actually gone. Desiring to hug her again, I longed for the human touch that only Mama could provide.

I felt an arm wrap around my waist as Joelle crept up alongside me pulling me in close. She knew how to love me tender as no else but Mama only could. There was a special closeness in our love that I know Mama sensed even before I did. It was her sixth sense that I believed Allie got from Mama. Mama had a special knack for seeing into one's soul discovering what resided within. Of course, what she saw in Dad's will always be a mystery to me but it was their love that made me possible. And for that, I was grateful.

Chapter 54

BLUE HAWAI'I

Joelle and I walked out to the edge of the property line overlooking the harbor. Reaching over I grabbed her hand slightly grazing her back end while attempting a romantic moment. She quickly slapped my hand away saying, "Stop trying to grab my butt Hackett. The kids might see."

"Dang woman, I was trying to hold your hand."

"Really? Of all times you want to honey up you pick now!"

"Well, all this talk of a secret society and your sexy title as The Chic Belle has gotten me feeling all sweet on you," I said while swiping her hand up in mine. "Baby love, it's like you've gotten your sexiness on and I'm feeling the sizzle coming from your frying pan."

"I need you to be serious for once in your life if that is even remotely possible for you to do. Do you understand the implications of what I've just told you?"

"I'm tracking with you baby. I really am."

"And boy, you had better not breathe a word of what I've said to anyone unless I give you express permission to do so.

You understand?!"

"I'm feeling you baby. I'm feeling you."

I think it was the combination of her serious tone and the tranquil Atlantic breeze that enabled me to keep my wits about me. But I also realized that the momentous occasion was certainly auspicious and our lives would forever change. So I responded the way any supportive, loving, and endearing husband would do in such a moment, "When do we start planning your Blue Hawai'i coronation, island style?"

"Funny you should ask, my love," Joelle replied with her trademark lazy smile. "We leave in a week for Kaua'i. The ceremony will take place on the very grounds where Elvis sang the Hawaiian Wedding Song in *Blue Hawai'i* and vacationed with Priscilla and their daughter Lisa Marie. The society will remember your Mama's contributions and service and then I will be inaugurated as her successor, the new TCB. We have first class tickets departing out of Memphis."

"Seriously?" I asked not believing what my ears were hearing.

"Oh yeah, as serious as the dark side of the moon," Joelle replied with an amused grin.

Beside myself with excitement, I had prayed for an opportunity like this. I spent a short stint over in Hawai'i back when I had graduated from high school. Kaua'i was where I proposed to Joelle. I couldn't help but wonder if there was more to this upcoming trip than just a gathering of The Blue Suede Purses.

Stepping closer to my sugar baby, I placed my hand around the small of her back and pulled her to me tightly. "Mama started something that was near and dear to her heart. I know she had her reasons for keeping things on a low. I'm all in. I'll be glad to head up your secret service. You need but say the word and I'll be mic'd and packing heat."

"Oh, my honey-wheat loaf of bread you're all the heat I'll ever need," Joelle said while leaning in to give me a kiss. It was a special moment for us, one inspired and made possible by the decision Mama made years earlier when she chose to begin the illustrious Blue Suede Purses.

We just lingered there for a moment arms around each other with Joelle's head leaning against my shoulder taking in the Charleston skyline amid the rosy sky backdrop of a setting sun. Our lives had indeed changed. We would continue what Mama had begun.

"The future is looking so bright I'll need to go buy a new pair of Ray-Bans," I said jokingly to Joelle. A peaceful, easy feeling came over me as the sun dipped from view. We were beginning a new chapter and one that would keep Mama's spirit alive and well.

Chapter 55

HACKETT'S VISION

Rising early the next morning, I hit the beach for a jog. What began as uneventful suddenly became anything but. Diving like a World War II era Corsair was a crazy seagull making a beeline in my direction. Hitting the sand hard as if assuming the position, all I could think was, *Dear God, it's a rabid gull?*

Rolling over quickly as the winged creature swooped by a hint of recognition came over me. It was Seagle. Standing up I followed his flight path watching intently as he turned back toward the direction I had been jogging.

And then he appeared out of the salty mist. At first as a silhouette against the first rays of dawn. Leaning on a short Rowan staff and robed in radiant white was none other than Rally, the sage raccoon spirit. Seagle arrested his descent and alighted on Rally's left shoulder.

Standing there in the sand, Rally stared in my direction with a mystical look across his bandit face. Transfixed by his gaze, his telepathic thought startled me. *Come closer, I won't bite.*

There was something different about Rally that I couldn't quite place. Maybe it was the context. Suddenly the wind began to whip around him but the sand did not stir. The waves like the sound of thunder were crashing upon the shore spitting water that did not touch him. Debris that had washed up on the beach including seaweed, sea glass, and sea oats, all began racing toward Rally in a violent collision course that he simply waved away with the swat of his paw. He seemed impervious to the elements as if totally at one with the essence of nature itself.

Seagle sat upon his shoulder with a reticent look on his ever-observant face unflustered by the swirling display of nature's power. I was astounded at their composure in the midst of such tornadic fury swirling chaotically around them. And then all became still almost unnaturally so, as if an unseen hand imposed a restraint over the elements with a power that only the supernatural can wield.

Breaking the eerie silence, Rally spoke with a sage voice. "Hackett, the Great Spirits wield power over the elements. In commanding the air, they bring restoring peace. In commanding the water, they wield the cleansing power of purity. In commanding the fire, they refine that which is corrupt. In commanding the earth, they breathe life into that which is lifeless. You have been chosen to receive a sacred gift which will be revealed in time. Use it wisely. And serve the Great Spirits well."

The last thing I remembered before I blacked out was Rally striking his Rowan staff on the sand eliciting a surging power that knocked me violently to the ground. The sounds of Kiwi cackling on the beach stirred me back to consciousness. The light of the morning sun reflected off the sand causing me to wince. I looked around for them but Rally and Seagle were gone. Down the beach I saw Kiwi running full speed along the hard packed sand filled with laughter as she cried out, "My goodness," with Queen Bean and Elvis in hot pursuit.

Sitting up on my elbows, I felt incredibly weak and yet at peace. If I had learned anything from that crazy raccoon, it was that the critter meant what he said and said what he meant. *Sacred gift*, I thought, curious as to exactly what it would be and used for what purpose. Not one who liked being left in the dark, I contented myself in knowing that all would be revealed in its own time. For now, I had something very important to do.

Chapter 56

DANCING IN THE FIRELIGHT

Gazing up at the crescent moon and then across the Charleston harbor I whispered quietly, "The Crescent Harbor", recalling Rally's words in my vision. He must've eavesdropped from Animora on one of the many conversations that Mama and I had while walking the harbor shores on many a night when the crescent moon cast it's captivating light down upon the harbor waters. Mama would often refer to the harbor on such enchanting nights as "The Crescent Harbor".

We gathered on the beach sitting on benches around a shallow fire pit that the kids and Elvis helped me carve out in the sand. Inside a ring of stones blazed a crackling bonfire. It was truly an enchanting evening beneath a dome of stars shining like sparkling diamonds providing celestial accents for a conspicuous crescent moon. The palmetto palms were gently swaying in the cool evening breeze. Filled with an overwhelming contentment, I found the auspicious evening perfect for scattering Mama's ashes where she grew up, enjoyed, and loved the most.

Louie ran over from the beach house carrying a bag of marshmallows and several camping forks. Bixie cast a devilish look Louie's way and said, "Really?" Kiwi jumped up with excitement at the thought of roasting marshmallows and excitedly ran over to grab an available camping fork.

I started to object but Joelle placed a hand on my knee signaling to allow the children their pleasure. And she was right because Mama would want her grandbabies to roast marshmallows to their little heart's content rather than sit around crying over her death. She was never one for all the pomp and circumstance that was often the case during a funeral service. Mama was very much a down-to-earth woman who enjoyed the simple pleasures in life like sitting around a bonfire on the beach enjoying the company of family and friends.

Starting off the informal celebration of Mama's life I gazed into the spitting fire and said, "Life is a gift that springs from the Giver of gifts. I give thanks to the Gift Giver who gave me the gift of Mama's love; the gift I will always cherish."

Louie jumped in before I could finish and said, "Ya-ya was funny."

I don't know if it was a sign from Mama but in that moment I could've sworn that I saw her silhouette dancing in the firelight. Her spirit was very much with us in a palpable way. Glancing over at Louie I continued, "You bet she was. Ya-ya gave the gift of funny!" Everyone sort of chimed in after that to contribute.

Kiwi was quick to add, "And ya-ya also gave the gift of happiness. I was always so happy around her."

In her soft-spoken, shy way Allie added, "Ya-ya saw dead animals." We all sort of looked her way at first thinking she was joking but something about her expression, which was straightforward, conveyed otherwise.

"You mean like road kill," I said, attempting to clarify.

"No. Ya-ya saw dead animals."

"I once had a cat named Misty. Well, after Misty died, I would often go to where we buried her and just spend hours talking to her. It is how I continued to feel close to Misty even though I could no longer hold her," Joelle said trying to illustrate what Allie was saying about Mama.

"But did Misty talk back?" Allie asked not taking her eyes away from the flames.

"No honey. Misty was dead."

"Well, ya-ya could hear the dead animals talk back. Especially Sam. She often talked to Sam."

"You mean her Siamese cat," Joel asked in amazement.

"Yes."

We all just sort of sat there in stunned silence considering the implications of what Allie had said. I was beginning to get the feeling that there was a lot more to Mama than I had realized. But it was all starting to make sense. My vision of Rally on the beach, the encounters with Buckminister, Squiditch, and Seagle. And even Elvis, her happenin' hound dog.

"Mama was a special lady. She loved animals with a special kind of love and they obviously, loved her back," I said as much for my own ears as for the ears of everyone seated around the fire pit. "The Great Spirits are made up not only of human spirits who have gone forth from this life to the next but also of sacred animal spirits who once walked this earth. We are joined with them not only in life but also in death."

There was a loud pop from within the fire pit that startled us. A chill swept down my spine as I was more aware than ever that we were not alone around that fire. The presence of the unseen was felt in a powerful way like I had never before experienced. Our imagination had been captured and stirred as we sat in silence each considering the words that Allie had shared. I was about to lean over to pick up Mama's blue suede purse when Bixie chimed in.

"I enjoyed shopping with ya-ya, especially on QVC. She didn't like buying cheap stuff and certainly didn't appreciate cheap gifts." Bixie probably imposed her own feelings with the last statement but I let it slide. "Ya-ya would often invoke the old Eddie Murphy joke when someone gave a cheap gift likening it to receiving a bottle of Brute by Faberje. And then she would say, "You cheap mother…"

I quickly jumped in before Bixie could finish the crass joke. "Ok then, well does anyone else have anything more to share regarding ya-ya before we scatter her ashes?"

"Yes. Annabelle was a dear soul. She gave me the gift of kindness. I pray all of us will be as kind as ya-ya was to others," Joelle said.

Kiwi and Louie cuddled closer to Joelle. "I miss ya-ya," Kiwi said with sadness in her voice. "Me too," Louie added. Allie just kept sucking her thumb while gazing into the fire very much engrossed in her mystical thoughts.

It was time. I reached over and picked up Mama's blue suede purse containing the plastic bag with her ashes in it. I stood and began the observance and celebration of scattering Mama's ashes signifying the return of her body to that from which it was made and to release her spirit in peace so that she could finally be free to soar beyond where the stars reside in the heavens.

Chapter 57

SAIL ON, SILVER GIRL

Removing the plastic bag containing Mama's ashes from her blue suede purse, the profound moment was not lost on any of us. I was holding in my hands the physical remains of Mama. Lifting her ashes up in the moonlight toward the crescent moon, I offered a prayer of thanksgiving to the Creator.

"Great Spirit of the living and of the dead, we salute you. From you, Mama received her spirit and back to you Mama's spirit has returned. From the dust of the earth you created the physical body. From the breath of your Spirit you breathed life filling our lungs with the air that surrounds us. From water you replenish all life. From fire you purify and refine all that is precious in your sight. You command the elemental powers that give and sustain life. We return the ashes of Mama's physical body back to the elements from which life was first constituted. Receive her spirit and permit her to take her place among the Great Spirits who have gone before. For the gift of her life we give thanks. Amen."

Everyone joined me in standing around the fire pit. Removing some ashes from inside the plastic bag, I tossed them into the flames. Passing the bag around, Joelle and the kids each tossed some of Mama's ashes into the flames representing the element of fire. We then walked over and scattered more ashes representing earth on the area of the beach where Mama used to sit enjoying the scenic beauty of the Atlantic Ocean and the Charleston Harbor. We then faced the easterly wind and tossed ashes into the breeze representing air. Finishing down by the shore, we waded into the shallows scattering more of Mama's ashes in the ocean representing water. We finished by washing our hands in the surf signifying the purification of flesh and spirit.

Standing beside me, Joelle put her arm around my back handing me Mama's blue suede purse to place Mama's remaining ashes for the trip to Graceland. Shuddering at the thought, I wondered what kind of trouble awaited us in Memphis. But there was no turning back now. If that's what Mama wanted then Elvis' grave was going to receive some rich fertilizer.

Kiwi walked over with her iTunes audio player connected to small speakers draped around her neck. She hit play so we could all listen to one of Mama's favorite songs *Bridge Over Troubled Waters.* Although Mama loved Elvis Presley's rendition the best, Kiwi chose the version by Andrea Bocelli and Mary J. Blige. And that was ok. Kiwi had a way of making her own what Mama had influenced in her. Mama would have it no other way.

I gave Joelle an affectionate squeeze around her waist as we both gazed out at the moon beams dancing upon the waters. It was a night filled with mystery and wonder. I couldn't help but feel connected to something larger than I had ever really believed existed. Where church religion had fallen flat for Mama and me, nature brought out the spiritual in us.

Releasing a contented sigh, I gazed toward the heavens marveling at the magnificence of the starry dome of God's grand cathedral. A thin trace of light suddenly lanced across the night sky inspiring a peace that Mama's spirit had finally crossed over. "Sail on, Silver Girl," I said as a tear tripped down my cheek.

How serene and eternal the heavens are, I thought. It was a night to remember. A night to be cherished. A night made possible by spirits both human and animal who carried out an audacious plan to switch Mama's ashes.

Epilogue

WHAT NOW MY LOVE?

The day started off normal enough. I had awakened refreshed and had enjoyed an exhilarating run along the beach. Joelle had the most scrumptious breakfast prepared and laid out buffet style on the wraparound porch. The kids were up and at em' busy around the table putting waffles, scrambled eggs, turkey sausage, and an assortment of strawberries, blackberries, and slices of honeydew melon on their plates.

Walking over I gave Joelle a peck on the cheek and a love pat on her booty which got Louie all stirred up by putting his face to the ground sticking his butt up in the air. "Alright boy. When I see a butt in the air, I will pop a butt in the air." Louie laughed and jumped back in his seat and began digging into the morning feast.

Kiwi glanced up from her plate and asked, "When are we going to put our Christmas tree up?" Due to Mama's passing and all the excitement surrounding it, our normal holiday routines were out of kilter.

"Yeah Dad. Christmas is only like two weeks away," Bixie said walking out onto the porch joining the rest of us. I could already see the bling, bling in her eyes and knew she was ready to transition into the season of giving. With everyone giving to her that is. But Bixie had a big heart in her own way. There's nothing she wouldn't do for you as long as there was some kind of benefit to be had in the giving.

Allie sat at the table and was sucking her thumb and twiddling her hair with her other hand. Strolling over, I planted a kiss on her head and said, "Love you sweetie." I proceeded to fill my plate when I heard my cell phone ringing back in the house.

"Dad, your phone is ringing," Louie hollered from his seat way over right next to me. "Ok, I hear it too," I yelled back while leaning over and pulling him close to give him a big old bear hug. We both shared a father and son moment in good humor. After giving him a peck on the forehead, I ran inside to answer my cell.

"Yello," I answered.

"Hackett, this is your brother Burt."

"What's up Burt?" He was sounding more like Dad the older he got.

"I'm afraid I have some sad news. It's about Dad." I froze afraid of what was coming next.

"Dad has gone on to be with Jesus. He had a heart attack

last night while visiting Mama's grave. The cemetery caretaker found him sprawled across her plot. Hackett, it couldn't have been scripted better almost as if Jesus had written it himself."

I felt suddenly numb and at a loss for words. Burt seemed to relish his next words, "I'm not sure if you realize it or not but Dad made me the executor of his last will and testament." I could detect the exultant tone in his voice.

Continuing Burt said, "Dad left instructions regarding his burial. He wishes to be buried next to Mama in the Historical Conundrum County Cemetery. I'd like for you to share a few words at the Memorial Service. Bishop JD will preside. I've already called and…" I simply clicked the phone off.

Joelle stepped inside immediately noticing the surreal expression settling on my weary face. "What is it honey?"

"It's Dad. He just died. And he's instructed that his ashes are to be buried next to Mama's in the Historic Conundrum County Cemetery."

Coming Soon – The Blue Suede Purses

Other Books By Holt Clarke

Visit HoltClarke.com

Visit HoltClarke.com

Visit HoltClarke.com

Visit HoltClarke.com

Visit KieraClarke.com

ABOUT THE AUTHOR

Holt Clarke is the father of the coolest kids on earth, on Santa's Nice List, and keep'n the magic real with his family in Charleston, South Carolina.

Holt earned the Doctor of Ministry degree from Drew University, Master of Divinity degree from Duke University, and Bachelor of Arts degree from North Carolina Wesleyan College.

Visit HoltClarke.com for news and updates.

www.ingramcontent.com/pod-product-compliance
Lightning Source LLC
Chambersburg PA
CBHW031239120726
47905CB00002B/660

* 9 7 8 0 9 9 7 9 8 8 8 0 2 *